To The

MW01591248

BLOOD MOON

Susan Jurgens Kammen

Shame on the Moon!

BLOOD MOON

Susan Jurgens Kammen

This novel is a work of fiction. Names, places, characters, and incidents are either the product of the author's imagination or are used fictitiously. Any references to real events, businesses, and locals are intended only to give the fiction a sense of reality and authenticity. Any resemblance to actual persons, living or dead is entirely coincidental.

All rights reserved. No part of this book may be reproduced or transmitted in any form or by any means, electronic or mechanical, including photocopying, recording, or by any information storage and retrieval system, without the written permission of the author.

Copyright © 2015 Susan Jurgens Kammen
All rights reserved.

ISBN: 1519297858
ISBN 13: 9781519297853

That the moon influences our behavior is an idea that appeals to us. Speak to law enforcement personnel or hospital employees and many will insist there is definitely a correlation between a full moon and human conduct. Many believe there are more accidents, violent incidents, and psychiatric admissions when a full moon fills the sky. Enter into that mix a Blood Moon and the tales become even more intriguing.

Blood Moon is dedicated to all who feel the effects of a full moon.

TABLE OF CONTENTS

"HOWLIN' AT THE MOON"

———

WHILE A FULL MOON SHINES brightly in the sky, an online rendezvous begins. Another victim's laundry would go unfolded, bills would be left unpaid, and conferences would be missed. People anonymously become intimate, at times exchanging sex for money or simply taking pleasure in arousing each other. One of the participants in a clandestine tryst will not leave the meeting; the encounter they had planned will turn into murder: hers.

CHAPTER 1

"IN DREAMS"

EMILY SEARCHED THROUGH THE BEDDING and the pile of papers on her bed. Her cell phone was ringing and interrupting her sleep. It was 2 a.m. and she was groggy. She checked her voice mail and heard a weak voice say, "Emme... Emme, is that you? Emme, I need you to come. Please come."

"Jenny?" Emily was sitting up now, wondering if it was a dream. Feeling dog tired, she flopped back into the soft bedding and quickly fell back to sleep.

She awakened at her usual time, 6:30 a.m., sat up, and talked to herself. "Okay, what happened last night? Did I actually get a phone call—from Jenny Westfield?" She talked to Rebel, the big orange cat she had adopted. The cat had come to her door on a gloomy October morning just as a cold rain had begun to fall. Emily was a sucker for animals, especially when it was chilly outside. She had scooped the soggy, frightened animal up and brought him inside. They had bonded quickly and now were roommates.

Emily checked the log on her cell phone. What she saw surprised her. There was no call last night—not from anyone, much less a dead person. Had she dreamed that her phone rang, that Jenny was calling her?

The voice on the phone had sounded eerily like Jenny's, her best friend from high school. But it couldn't have been. Dear sweet Jenny had been dead for many years. It had to have been a dream.

Emily's thoughts were now all about Stonebridge, the resort Jenny's family owned. She thought of that beautiful place often but hadn't seen anyone from the resort in years. Emily's family's summer cabin sat on what was once the lot at the end of the exclusive resort. The resort had eventually swallowed up their summer get-away, and Emily's father would occasionally get offers from the resort to purchase the now highly valued 150-foot lot. Emily, her father's personal representative, had ignored the offers and the sometimes-extreme pressure from the attorney for the resort.

Emily began her day with her usual sliced apple and a big bowl of oatmeal. It would hold her until her lunch meeting today with a finicky client. Her first stop would be the fabric shop where the owner, who had worked with Emily for years, would have an abundant array of material and paint samples in stock.

An eight-hour workday was never long enough for all Emily had to accomplish; too soon, night had swallowed the day. Exhausted, she was, as usual, ready for a good night's sleep.

Her phone again awoke her at 3:00 a.m. She was quick to answer this time. She groggily uttered, "Hello."

"Emme?" The voice, sounding like Jenny's, was weak—just a whisper. "Emme, I need you…you need to come. You need to tell."

Click.

Before Emily could respond, the call had ended. She was completely awake and quickly checked her phone log, but again there had been no call. "Guess it was a dream," she murmured, her thoughts again of Jenny. Over and over, she puzzled out Jenny's words from her dream. She wasn't really spooked by the dream nor by the words asking her to come home. But "to tell"…*to tell what*, she wondered.

Emily and Jenny had been best friends. Emily worked in her father's lumberyard; but when she wasn't working, she and Jenny were together. Their summer evenings were filled with swimming, fishing, and water skiing. Jenny taught swimming lessons to resort customers, and Emily would help Jenny with the hotdog and marshmallow roasts. Emily closed her eyes, and, for just a second, she was back on the beach with Jenny.

Emily searched through her phone for the number of another long ago friend, Sarah Hardy, who was soon answering.

"Hi, Emily! Oh my gosh, I can't believe it's really you." As they talked about their old friendship and how much time had passed, Sarah brought up the upcoming all-school reunion, reminding Emily that a letter had been sent to her. "Maybe you didn't get the paper work to fill out or lost track of it." Sarah talked fast, just as she had when they were young and saw each other almost every day. "Anyway…just please come. Everyone is excited to see you."

"Yeah, right…," Emily thought to herself but said, "Oops, gotta go, I'll talk to you later."

Speaking to her pillow, Emily muttered, "Everyone's excited to see me? Sure!" Emily socked her pillow with her fist, then shut off her phone and sank into the pillows and blankets. She rolled over, tucked the quilt under her chin, and remembered the last time she had seen Sarah. It was the after-graduation party at Jess's cabin. Images of drinking and casual sex filled her head. She stopped herself when a picture of Scott Turner, naked from the waist down, burbled up. She threw back her covers and headed for a cold shower. *What was I thinking? Who was I then?*

Emily's rebellious behavior had started after Jenny drowned. The therapist, however, had pressed hard for other aspects of her life, not convinced the death of her dear friend was the only trigger in her unruly behavior. She had asked herself those same questions over the last several years, but there was never an answer. Her therapist had grilled her: Had she been molested as a child? Had she been date raped? Had she used drugs?

Emily was honest and answered every question. Her father was a gentle, caring man. He never abused her or her brother in any way. He was a good provider. She loved her father and tried hard to remember other men who had been in their home or in her life growing up, but there were no memories of abuse. She had been involved with the drinking scene; and, for a brief, chaotic time, she had dabbled in drugs. They even tried hypnosis to get at suppressed memories, but nothing was found to explain why this pretty, bright young woman should have become so promiscuous. She had been rebelling for a reason, but that explanation was not forthcoming. Despite her behavior, her grades had been good, and she had graduated with honors.

Emily dried herself and felt a little better. The shower had cleared her head, and she again tucked conscious memories safely away. Her therapist had taught her to slip unhappy thoughts into a secure place in her mind where they wouldn't abruptly surface and ruin her day.

Emily searched her bookcase. The 1995 yearbook still felt new. She had hardly looked at the pages since getting it almost 20 years ago. A few of them stuck together, and the pages still smelled of ink.

Her therapist would have Emily recount her school activities and talk about her classes, hoping to find positive memories to add balance to Emily's recollections—for her sake. Emily was bright and had been involved in many activities, even in charge of several. The boys had liked her; the girls probably had not.

"I had sex with the whole football team," she said with a pathetic laugh, but there was no pleasure in the sex, or humor. She had been used, and she knew it. Back then it didn't matter. She needed their affection, but why, she now wondered. It wasn't really the whole team, but it felt like it had been. She had read enough and had been through a sufficient amount of therapy to know she had acted out to be noticed, to be hugged and held by someone—anyone.

Emily reached over to pick up the picture she had by her bed. As she took a long, sentimental look at the handsome man smiling back at her, she began to sob. Once a tall, dignified man, he was now frail and slight—his six-foot frame had shrunk several inches and his memory was sporadic from a stroke. Her father had been her rock—her protector. He had been strapped into his wheelchair and confined to the nursing home, his days were filled with instructions from the caregivers. "Take your pill, Mr. Blake." "Here's a drink of water, Sweetie." "Oh, good job, Paul. You ate all your dinner." How humiliating for such a once-capable man.

Emily had watched an aide spoon-feed him pea soup as he choked and tried to spit it out. She gagged, watching the aide cajole and persuade.

Finally, unable to control herself, she had verbally lashed out at the young girl. Planting herself between the aide and her father, she had pushed the food away.

Okay, I was a little aggressive, she had admitted to herself.

Her father had recuperated remarkably well and had moved into a luxurious senior living complex.

There was actually a reason to go back other than the mysterious phone-call dream and the all-school reunion. The renter in her father's cabin was moving out, and it was time to put the lake place up for sale. Stonebridge had been ready for years to buy the old cabin; Emily was quite sure it had become an eyesore for them.

Emily would have the task of cleaning the cabin out and disposing of personal items. She already knew she would have to do it alone. Her brother, Josh, wouldn't take any responsibility for the cabin or their belongings still packed away in the attic.

Emily had called Josh many times over the last years to ask for help with the house or their father. If he was sober enough to talk, he was irritated and rude to her. She used to ask him what was wrong. Why was he mad at her? They had been close as children. Only 16 months apart, they were always together, running to the park for a picnic or swimming in the lake. The question of what drove them apart had become something she no longer thought about much.

"He has something stuck somewhere that he is still steaming over. I wish I knew and maybe we could work it out," Emily had said so many times when she first left home. Friends also wondered why Josh had cut her out of his life: they had been so close, but no one knew the answer. Only once did she get somewhat of a response from him. He was intoxicated and slurred his words as he stood close to her. "We are such cowards. How can we live with ourselves?"

"Cowards?" Emily had screamed at him. "What are you talking about?"

Josh had staggered away into the night, and that was the last time they had spoken.

She had played her life over a million times. Emily couldn't imagine why he had referred to them as cowards.

"Maybe this time," she said to Rebel, as the cat rubbed against her leg. "Maybe this trip home will be the right time to talk."

Emily made a call to her therapist. She would need to see her and talk about a few things before her trip. She must have sounded stressed as the receptionist found time for her the very next day.

CHAPTER 2

"THAT'S WHAT IT'S LIKE TO BE LONESOME"

———◆———

EMILY HAD A HOUSE TO decorate. Her business kept her busy and gave her a good living. She loved making a room come alive. "It's your home," she would tell the uneasy homeowner. "It should reflect *your* tastes and *your* passions."

Emily would show pictures to her clients and bring a wide range of carpet, paint, wall coverings, tile, and wood flooring samples. She would talk with them about their dreams for their homes, how they would like to feel when they entered a room. Although trends in the decorating industry came and went much like clothing fashions, different areas of the country also had fads mixed in with long lasting traditions.

When Emily met with a client, she asked a variety of questions, which would give her an idea of what would make the home uniquely theirs. Clients were as different as snowflakes. Some were timid, wanting Emily to make the decisions for them. Others were bold and forthright... but often aesthetically off. Emily had a subtle way of discovering what their likes and dislikes were, and homes were soon reflecting distinct personalities. They seemed surprised and delighted with her uncanny expertise.

Emily had truly found her niche and loved her work. She would often remind herself of a quote she had heard: "If you love your job, you will never work a day in your life." She knew that was true because she was excited to wake everyday with the thought of another home to decorate. Emily arrived at the enchanting home she had been hired to redo. She had taken on the responsibility with some hesitation. The owner, an ageing actress from the 1970s, was known for being difficult with anyone who worked for her. Emily had cajoled and catered to her for many months. This, however, was the day of reckoning. Fabrics, furniture, and paint would either be ordered that day, or Emily was finished with the old woman. A contractor and Emily had worked closely to put this all together. They had drawn up a plan that included relocating walls and windows. That phase had been acceptable and was almost complete. However, her client continually placed Emily's designs on hold.

As always, when she drove up to the mansion, she was awed by the view. The estate was set prominently on an elevated lot and was surrounded by stunning mountainous scenery.

She had designed a chandeliered foyer as the gateway to a dramatic dining room and a magnificent heart-of-the-home circular family room. A huge, curved wall of nearly floor-to-ceiling windows that showcased endless panoramas graced this sun-splashed area. A seamless pathway led to the fabulous kitchen, outfitted with handsome alder cabinetry and desert-hued granite countertops. It was furnished with state-of-the-art appliances.

Tucked in the far wing of the house, the master suite boasted a blissful bedroom with expansive picture windows, a sunny sitting area, an exercise room, and a luxurious bath with a jetted tub and a walk-in block glass shower. A semi-circular hallway led to the other bedrooms; each would be decorated in different themes, yet accenting the grand, rugged terrain.

Welcomed by Rita, Sybil Fitzgerald's longtime personal assistant, Emily drank coffee with her thorny client. She stated her need to have a commitment to her decorating ideas because she would be leaving for Minnesota soon. To her delight, the client gave the go-ahead. Emily would have no difficulty in ordering the materials and furniture needed now, and then winding up the project after her trip home. She and Sybil sealed their contract with coffee, a scone, and signed contracts.

Sybil Fitzgerald had no one. Her four husbands' mottos, so to speak, had been Use and Abuse. One husband had died while they were still married; and she frankly wished the others had, too. However, a young, debonair man with whom she had had a steamy, illicit affair had given her a child—a daughter—the only person in this world she had truly loved. For a time, she and her ToyBoy were the talk of Hollywood, which had damaged her career; she was considered box office poison.

Sybil's lovely daughter, Tina, had walked on the wild side. She had been a spirited young woman who had occasionally dabbled in rough sex. One rainy spring morning, she had failed to come home. When Tina had been missing for three days, her mother called the police. She had to acknowledge her daughter's lifestyle, so the police didn't seem too concerned about the missing girl. She had just turned 18 and was an adult. The police did learn, however, that Tina had emptied the substantial trust fund her father had established for her. Sybil was devastated.

A large, stunning portrait of Tina hung over the fireplace in the living room. Her mother pointed out the exotic features of this beauty. "She looks like her father," Sybil said with pride. She said in a hushed tone, "I just wish I could find her. I know in my heart she's dead but would like to set her spirit free."

Emily hugged the frail woman and walked to her car. *Everyone has a story,* she thought. *We need to listen to understand.* But for now, she was off to place orders and make travel arrangements. Direction and resolution energized her; she actually looked forward to the trip to Minnesota.

While Emily prepared for her journey back home, law enforcement and family plotted to revive a horrible memory they believed might be buried deep in Emily's mind. The shuffling of chairs was the only noise in the courthouse meeting room. Gathered for their meeting were Sheriff Emerson, the local police chief, Paul Blake (Emily's father), Billie Westfield, and Kirsten Graham (a representative from the

Minnesota Bureau of Criminal Apprehension). Stone de'Buhr had also been asked to be a part of this discussion. He sat silently in the back of the room.

"I called her last night...and the night before," Kirsten said. The pretty detective from the BCA had a few things to tell the group. She said she had also been able to remove the calls from Emily's cell phone log so there was no record that calls had come in.

"I don't like doing this," Kirsten said calmly but firmly. "We're trying to make Emily think Jenny's spirit is talking to her from the grave. This is a woman you all think is dealing with a repressed, violent memory. I can't help but ask myself if we aren't contributing to her problems. Perhaps it will be *our* behavior that sends her mind into oblivion."

Paul rubbed his forehead and then asked the county attorney if he was sure Emily knew something about Jenny's death. The death had been ruled an accidental drowning, but there were rumors.

The sheriff said, "We think they both know—both Emily and your son—but we have no proof—nothing but a hunch, a gut feeling, and some notes written by a member of the search party at the time of the drowning. Rescue crews had found Jenny's body in a large patch of weeds, which could have tangled up around her neck; but the man who actually discovered the body stated that it looked as if her neck had been slashed. Her death was, however, ruled a drowning by the medical examiner."

"They may *not* remember what *we* think they may have seen," Billie added. Their thinking was that bringing Emily back to the area of Jenny's death might trigger helpful memories to surface.

The sheriff went on to say that some of the notes in the file were not accurate. In addition to the mystery of Jenny's death, three other young women were also missing. He noted that two of them had disappeared when there was a full moon. The third one had not; there had been only a sliver of moon the night that she disappeared.

To this, Billie said that many believe the moon pulls on the psyche of certain personalities. "Law enforcement personnel or hospital employees and others," she said, "insist there is a correlation between a full moon and human behavior." She continued, "A blood moon adds even greater suspicion that people engage in crazy, wild behavior." She added that although researchers can't prove that behavior is affected, some people working during the wee hours of the night even believe a blood moon causes a Werewolf Syndrome.

Billie gave a subtle nod to Stone who was sitting quietly in the back of the room; he had come back to help her run the resort. They were all aware of the suspicion surrounding him: Each missing woman had last been seen with him. It had been a long time since he had been home and many years since the women had vanished. They had never been found, yet he had never been charged with anything. Law enforcement believed someone was trying to frame him.

Billie had a degree in psychology but had not worked in that arena for years. While she wanted to glean information from Emily and Josh, she argued intently that pressure must be carefully applied. No one wanted Emily or Josh pushed over the edge.

Billie had married and worked at the family resort for the last several years. "Josh has something going on. His binge drinking is certainly over some kind of trouble in his life."

"There's an all-school reunion coming up, too," the young woman from the BCA remarked. "That may bring her home."

"That's fine," Paul said, finally speaking up. "But we need something to keep her here for a while." Paul had a sad look on his face as he conspired with law enforcement to trap his daughter and son into disclosing a painful old memory.

"Emily's an interior decorator," Billie reminded them. "I could hire her to redo some of the older cabins at the resort. They certainly need it, and the project would require her to stay awhile."

Kirsten offered, "Stone and I are spending time together. It's an alibi for him should he need it. We also hope that if there is a person out there trying to frame him, I'll be the one he...or she...goes after." Her matter-of-fact tone was noticeable. She went on to say that the undercover receptionist job she had at Stonebridge was fun—interesting and so different from her normal duties as an investigator for the BCA, and that she and Stone were becoming friends although, she quickly added, they were not interested in each other romantically.

CHAPTER 3

"Red Necks, White Socks, and Blue Ribbon Beer"

—————◆—————

JOSH STUMBLED INTO THE BATHROOM, turned on the shower, and stepped in. The icy water took his breath away. He vaguely recalled the fight he had been in the night before. His left eye was swollen, and his lip bled as the water hit it. He had made a pact with himself that he would not go into the Nip and Sip ever again. That however hadn't stopped him from following Ned into the smelly establishment and fighting with the three city slickers standing at the bar.

The arrogant strangers were in the north woods to fish, sporting expensive gear and attire. Sticking out like sore thumbs, they strutted their stuff while looking down at the locals as country hicks.

Belittling the waitresses was the beginning of the visiting sportsmen's demise. Granted, the locals slapped the waitresses' bottoms and told the young women a few off-color jokes, but that was their so-called right. They lived here; this was their territory. The hometown men did not appreciate interlopers despite their bringing business to the local economy. Josh knew before the day was over he'd most likely have a visit from the police.

Attired in suit, tie, and cleanly shaved, Josh looked like any one of those businessmen. His job at the bank had been given to him when he married Holly. He had a head for banking and was a trusted member of the staff. Holly Abbott Blake was born into wealth, and Josh continued to benefit from their marriage even though his behavior was appalling at times. He could go months or more sober, but he was a binge drinker. Never knowing what might set him off was the scariest part of his addiction. Holly's uncle, Brian, chastised Josh about his drinking and threatened to fire him, but Josh wasn't worried. Holly's mother owned part of the bank; and, although she had become extremely odd, she would never allow her grandchildren's father to be fired.

Josh would sleep off the effects of drinking in a cabin built on their sprawling property. There his hangovers would not interfere with their daily lives and inevitable arguments could be kept away from the children. Josh had been a bright boy and a responsible man. What happened to send him into the abyss of binge drinking was a mystery to his family and friends. Although his mother had been plagued by a gambling addiction and had died young, his father was a respected man in the community, having started a lumberyard with his friend Jack that now covered an entire block, as well as four other lumberyards in surrounding communities.

Sleet was pecking on the bedroom window when Holly's alarm went off. As she awoke, she realized that Josh hadn't come to their bed last night. He must be at the cottage—their *safe house*; at least she hoped he had made it that far. He had never driven home after a night of drinking, so she hoped that bit of good judgment had continued. Someone always took care of him when he was incapable of watching out for himself. Josh's drinking problems often lead to other difficulties, like fights in a bar. He was liked by many though—troubles and all. Holly had loved him since seventh grade. He could go for long periods of time without drinking, but when the floodgates opened, his cravings sent him awash.

The children were off on the bus to school, and Holly walked into the clinic to start her working day. She was a nurse for one of the doctors. Their day usually started with phones ringing and patients sitting in their cars, waiting for the doors to open. Holly had started her nursing career working in a hospital. After their first child was born, she took this job, needing the more regular hours of a clinic. Although Josh didn't drink every night, she still couldn't count on him always to be responsible and home with the children.

Holly also had her mother on her mind almost every day. Her mother's hoarding and age crept into her thoughts so often these days. What would happen if her mom got hurt or ill? Holly had tried everything she could think of to help. Her father had, too, until Roxanne's hoarding drove him to divorce her.

Holly had enough to worry about. Josh had indeed made it to the cottage after his night of binge drinking, and her mom was safe, at least for right now. She had a job to do.

Holly had already begun to look at other career options. The healthcare industry had changed over the years, and RNs working in a hospital setting rarely practiced caring for the patients, bogged down instead with administrative details. Actual hands-on care had been mostly delegated to aides and technicians. One-to-one interaction for an RN with patients was a rarity. Yet, nurses were still in demand, and there would be a shortage over the next years. Moreover, an aging population would constitute a great need for medical personnel trained in geriatrics to work in outpatient settings. Although doctors were still thought of as the primary care providers, many nurse practitioners were providing services once reserved exclusively for doctors. Maybe more school would be a good idea, she thought. She liked the hours of the clinic but eventually her children would be older and finding their own way in life and careers. She and Josh would be empty nesters.

Another valued option for RNs was to become certified life care planners, which Holly researched. She had attended seminars to learn about the services a life plan could provide. Nurses who chose this path worked with elderly or terminally ill patients and their families to ensure that a program of quality healthcare was in place.

As she called the next patient to see Dr. Lundy, she recognized Stone de'Buhr. He was sitting in the waiting room with his sister. Holly knew Billie had been ill and that tests were still being run to diagnose the problem. Holly loved Billie and remembered when her mom and Billie had been close friends. That closeness had ended when her mother's hoarding took control. Her father had left when she was in her senior year of high school. He had remarried and seemed happy with his new wife. Holly had made many attempts to help her mom get control of her illness but the monster had power over everything in Roxanne's life. Nothing her family or friends could do or say could change the power of her addiction. Holly couldn't believe her mother would rather have her *stuff* around her than her daughter and family.

Holly turned her attention to Billie and Stone. The doctor would see them, and Holly showed them to the examining room. Taking Billie's blood pressure, making friendly chit chat with her and Stone, Holly tried to assess the relationship between Billie and her much younger brother and also asked some personal questions. Her file showed a variety of tests; but nothing was telling them why she was feeling ill. Billie's problem seemed intermittent, good days followed by debilitating ones. After the usual blood pressure check and review of Billie's medications, Holly told Billie the doctor would be with her shortly. There was definitely something wrong.

CHAPTER 4

"SENTIMENTAL JOURNEY"

———◆———

EMILY DROVE HER LEXUS DOWN the long road that led to the exclusive resort. Was she being pretentious by renting a luxury car? Not really, she
told herself. That's what she had back home and that's what she would
have been driving had she decided to take a road trip instead of flying
home.

Mature trees now formed a canopy over most of the road, forming an
impressive archway. The closer to Stonebridge she drove, the more perfectly trimmed hedges she saw lining the driveway. Flower gardens and
large fountains invited people to enjoy the beauty of the surroundings.
A huge sign welcomed visitors to the popular resort. Soon Stonebridge
came into view—a wonder to behold.

The driveway that led to the Blake's cabin was just a short distance
from the lodge. To the left and down the paved road, it really stood
out. It was an old-style log chalet and looked more rustic and rundown
than she had remembered. *No wonder they want to buy it,* she thought. It
looked pitiful among the other remodeled and newer buildings. There
were condos across the road with impressive landscaping and walking
paths, but there stood the old, decrepit cabin. She laughed out loud as
she thought of it as a cabin; Billie de'Buhr Westfield must have thought
of it as an unwanted stepchild.

A tall man with a plaid work shirt and jeans saw Emily drive in and
walked over to the car to ask if he could help her. He was pleasant, and

she told him who she was, explaining that she was the owner of the cabin. He nodded his assent.

Emily's key opened the door with ease. The cabin smelled of fish, stale air, and mold. She opened the windows and let memories of the place cascade over her. Tears welled up in her eyes, which she wiped away with the sleeve of her shirt. She had redone this cabin a hundred times in her mind. Over the last years, she had dreamed of coming back and rejuvenating their summer place. It held so many cherished memories. She smiled at the image she caught of herself in the streaked and scratched front room mirror. Tears continued to stream, running in her makeup.

Everything was old and looked worse than she had remembered. They had a renter for many years, and obviously he had not cared how the cabin looked. Emily was surprised he hadn't called to demand they put new furniture in and update the appliances.

She would talk things over with her dad. It would be up to him if they sold. Although he had given Emily his power of attorney when he had his stroke, he was better now and quite capable of making decisions. Emily would like to keep the cabin, but that, too, would take a lot of money and time. It really wouldn't be livable unless they spent a lot to upgrade it. The structure may not even be sound anymore, in which case it would have to be taken down. A new cabin would be expensive, and building a new one would irritate the Stonebridge owners who wanted to buy the old one and make it part of the resort.

Emily just wished she could call Josh and invite him over to revisit all the wonderful times they once had here. Emily knew that would never happen. Josh had cut her off years ago without so much as a word about why. Instead, she was plagued with why he thought they were cowards.

Emily unpacked her clothes. She had tried to pack lightly, as she hoped to shop in the local stores in Hidden Rapids. There she would find the trappings of northern Minnesota. Garments with wolf, loon, duck, and deer motifs would be easily found on a sweatshirt, tee shirt, or jacket. She also found a place for an icon of sorts she always kept

near—a plaque with Thomas Jefferson's "Ten Rules for the Good Life."
She smiled at the advice:

1. *Never put off 'til tomorrow what you can do today.*
2. *Never trouble another for what you can do yourself.*
3. *Never spend your money before you have it.*
4. *Never buy what you do not want because it is cheap; it will never be dear to you.*
5. *Pride costs us more than hunger, thirst, and cold.*
6. *Never repent of having eaten too little.*
7. *Nothing is troublesome that we do willingly.*
8. *Don't let the evils that have never happened cost you pain.*
9. *Always take things by their smooth handle.*
10. *When angry, count to 10 before you speak; if very angry, count to 100.*

Feeling weary and a bit overwhelmed by all the memories, Emily decided a swim was exactly what she needed. The cabin was stuffy and hot, but a dip in the lake would cool her off. There was no air conditioning in the cabin, and the fan that had been there for years made a horrible squeaking sound. She knew it would be particularly irritating tonight when she tried to sleep.

As she ambled her way to the beach, she glanced at the lodge. It had been beautifully landscaped and looked more like a castle than a northern lodge. Looking up at the fourth floor, she felt panicky: her stomach hurt and her breath came faster. The feeling disappeared as quickly as it had come. *What's that about?* she wondered.

The water looked inviting, and she walked into the still chilly lake. Her strong breaststroke moved her quickly into the middle where the current was fighting against her. It was overwhelming. She enjoyed the pool in her condo complex almost every day, but it certainly wasn't like this. She had forgotten how difficult it had been to pit herself against the power of the ever-changing Pokegama. The current where the

Mississippi River coursed through the lake was a quiet demon, appearing calm and inviting, yet quickly turning with brute force against a swimmer.

She wasn't that out of shape—or was she? Panic was beginning to overpower her. *Okay, settle down*, she told herself. *Get a grip—don't panic—you can do this.* She reminded herself of the strength she used to have. She knew it was still there. Emily thought back on her days as an athlete in high school and college where she surprised her coaches with the power of her small, slight body. She reminded herself of all the hours she and Jenny had spent in the water, pushing themselves to the limits of their endurance, each helping the other press on despite aching arms and legs.

Suddenly there she was—Jenny—with her powerful strokes, swimming right next to Emily. With disbelief Emily pushed harder, unexpectedly stronger, and she felt secure in her ability to survive. Although her muscles hurt, they were still working for her, and she was getting ever closer to the shore. As the water became calmer, Jenny was gone. Emily was surprised and sad. She had truly seen her friend—in fact, had even touched her arm as they surged through the lake.

When she reached the shore, she collapsed on the sand. When she finally got her breath back, she spoke out loud. "What was that?" she asked. "Was Jenny with me—was she a ghost—a spirit?" Jenny had been there, swimming with her, giving her strength, and pushing her on, saving her life.

Tears flowed as she thought of Jenny. They had spent so much time in the lake. They had felt they were conquering, even taming, the powerful Pokegama. Jenny had come back to save her life. She believed it—she knew it.

As she lay on the warm sand, she realized a man was looking down at her. Stone de'Buhr stood over her, smiling. "I saw you struggling in the water and was about to come out with the boat."

"Did you see anyone with me?" Emily asked, squinting into the sun.

"No. I didn't see anyone. Weren't you out there alone?"

"Yes, yes I was," Emily stammered, looking away. She certainly didn't want him to think she was crazy. "But thank you for at least thinking of saving me," she said.

"I wouldn't have let you drown. I do remember what a super athlete you were—as was Jenny. It's hard to believe she could drown—strong swimmer that she was. I guess it just goes to show we can all fail if the situation is right."

Stone reached down and helped Emily get up. "We're having a party tonight to start the week off for the new guests," he said. "Won't you join us?"

"I'm really not a guest. I don't know if your sister would like it."

"She would love it, and, yes, you are a guest even if you don't feel like it. You were my niece's best friend, remember?"

"Okay, I'll be there. What time does it start?"

Stone told her to come about 5:00 or when she saw the gathering begin.

As she made her way back to her cabin, the realization of what had happened on the lake hit her. She could have died out there, and maybe that's exactly what happened to Jenny. She must have been caught off guard— just like Emily had been. She and Jenny had experienced the thrashing that Pokegama could unleash on an unsuspecting swimmer. Emily reminded herself that they had each become seasoned swimmers over the years and had felt confident in their abilities. But, that was a long time ago when she and Jenny had been well conditioned, strong, and young.

As she showered, the squealing noise hurt her ears, so she hurried, realizing she needed to have that showerhead replaced, too. She dried her hair, pulled it back into a ponytail, added a pretty pink lipstick, and walked to the beach area just down from the lodge.

CHAPTER 5

"SUMMERTIME"

———◆———

THE BRIGHT ORANGE SETTING SUN and clear blue lake water soothed Billie as she sipped a refreshing drink. While relaxing from a busy day at the resort and looking at the beach, she could see Murphy, their yellow Lab, also calming down after a day full of activity. It was Sunday night, and new customers had been registering all afternoon. It would take Murphy a day to get used to the new people and stop feeling protective of the family. He was a friendly dog but still watchful. He had never been aggressive. However, there had been times when the hair on the back of his neck stood up as he softly growled, barely audible. Stone had just stuck his head into the lodge and told Billie he had invited Emily to join them for the Sunday night welcome party.

Beatrice ("Billie") de'Buhr was born into a wealthy southern family who had come from France in the early 1800s and had settled in Louisiana. Her life had been one of privilege and gracious living. Her father had invested in logging in northern Minnesota and had also bought the beautiful Baycliffe mansion. Stonebridge, as it was now called, was nestled into the lush landscape of northern Itasca County on Pokegama Lake. Baycliffe had been a unique estate. It wasn't far from town but it was a million miles away in luxury. Baycliffe had been a 45-acre property with 2,000 feet of lakeshore south of Hidden Rapids. The owner had been a real-estate mogul from New York. He and his family had used it as a summer home until he died and his wife remarried. It was then put up for sale and de'Buhr Properties purchased it. Billie's mother, wanting something to occupy her time while her husband was off making money, decided to turn part of the property into a resort.

They changed the buildings that housed employees into cabins and the main house into a lodge. The huge dining room and kitchen could easily handle a large number of guests. In time, the mansion and property became a prized vacation retreat.

A tag-a-long brother named Stone was soon intruding on Billie's life. As Billie's mother cradled her newborn son, Billie had felt suddenly alone and left out. She smiled now, remembering the day Stone was born. When he was delivered, he had dark unruly hair, a wrinkled red face, and belted out a cry that startled even those in the surrounding rooms. However, this baby brother, who Billie had seen as an interloper, soon captured her heart.

Billie had a quietly beautiful face with dark brown eyes, and a robust figure. Two young girls— Roxanne and Charlotte—had taken Billie under their wings and helped her adjust when the family decided to make the move to Hidden Rapids permanent. They had been considered popular in high school, and their acceptance paved the way for Billie to be welcomed into the community. The three soon became inseparable.

They had all joined the swim team in high school and were instrumental in their school's ascent into the halls of Minnesota state swimming fame. In later years, Billie and Charlotte's daughters would follow that same path and become even better swimmers. Sadness swept over Billie for a few minutes as she remembered her beloved Jenny, her beautiful graceful daughter who had succumbed to the turbulent water of Pokegama soon after bringing home a state swimming trophy for her school.

Billie thought nostalgically of her two high school friends. Billie, Charlotte, and Roxanne had been as close as sisters. They had been athletic and popular. Swimming had been their sport, and they had excelled in an activity that demanded strength and agility. They had been called the three mermaids by the newspaper and the name stuck.

Pictures of the three were often on the sports page of the Herald Review and occasionally in the Minneapolis Star and Tribune.

Charlotte had met a handsome man a few years older than she was. He wanted to marry as soon as she finished high school. Despite her parents' objections, they married and began to try for a family. When Charlotte didn't get pregnant right away, she fell into a depression. Her husband, Paul, tried to assure her that it would happen; it would just take a little more time. Trips to the doctor did not seem to help. Gambling at the local casino seemed to be the one thing that eased her concern and gave her something else to think about. Charlotte won money at times, which fueled her addiction.

After a few years, she did become pregnant, and Paul hoped that would straighten out their lives. But her gambling addiction had become her selfish lover. The obsession seemed to lessen somewhat while she carried her child, and she became devoted to the little girl she named Emily Rose. Months went by, and Paul felt a sense of relief. Caring for her daughter seemed to fill the space formerly spent gambling. Life for the couple and newly formed family felt secure and happy.

A son they named Josh came along before Emily had turned two. Their family was complete, and Charlotte had managed to control her addiction for the first years of her children's lives. However, the jealous lover soon took over again, and Charlotte lapsed into the quagmire.

Billie had met and began dating Jim her sophomore year in college. They fell in love but waited to marry until both had graduated. Billie and Roxanne had gone to the same college, and each had graduated with degrees in psychology. Intent on saving the world, they were going to help everyone have a better life. Their Masters Degrees from the University of Minnesota-Duluth and their supervised work under a psychologist in Hidden Rapids led to buying his practice when he retired.

Jim had a position with the Minnesota Department of Natural Resources; but, when Billie's father was diagnosed with cancer, he resigned to run Stonebridge, the family resort. Billie's arthritic mother helped until she was unable to walk without a walker.

Billie and Roxanne continued with their careers until Roxanne's hoarding claimed control of her life. No one, including Billie, could help her. She had become unable to fulfill her duties as a partner in their clinic. Billie couldn't handle it alone, and the work at the resort was more than Jim could handle, even with Stone's help and their many employees. They had needed a leader, and that leader was Billie.

A knock on the door and a brief word from Stone let Billie know their guests were arriving. The smell of beef cooking on the grills and fires in the fire pits gave off an ambience that let everyone know they had arrived at the beach. Soft sand and delicious food offered the guests, young and old, the beginning of what would be a memorable week at the lake.

Emily received a hard, genuine hug from Billie. Although Billie and her mother, Charlotte, had been the best of friends and likewise Emily and Jenny, there seemed to be some animosity toward the Blake's with their refusal to sell the old cabin to Stonebridge. Regardless, they wolfed down food and drink, and then settled on chairs and benches around the fire, singing familiar songs to the accompaniment of one of the guests, strumming his guitar.

Stone and his friend Kirsten had stayed close to Emily all evening; and, as she stood up to leave the cozy fire, he asked if he and Kirsten could walk her back to her cabin. "Yes, thank you," she answered with a wide smile, taking his outstretched arm. The three ambled their way up the slight hill to her place. Stone hugged her good night. "We'll see you tomorrow," he said, waving as he and Kirsten walked back down the hill toward the fire. Kirsten and Stone looked and acted like a couple in love.

Billie was busy cleaning up after the gathering. She was satisfied with the way the welcome party had gone. She loved a new batch of customers. She had redone the website for the resort many times. She wanted it to look perfect so readers could easily see what Stonebridge had to offer. They never had trouble filling their cabins and lodge suites; but competition was keen, and many new resorts were being built around the popular lake area. The large welcome party was proof her efforts had paid off.

CHAPTER 6

"Tossing and Turning"

———◆———

Stone pulled the covers back and crawled into bed. He had slept in this room from birth until he left for college. The window by the bed afforded a view of 30 boats tied up in the harbor and the pristine swimming beach. Memories of the lake were pleasant. No, they had been wonderful until he left for college. From then on, his returns had been plagued with trouble. Why his returning home would correlate with the disappearance of young women was a perplexing problem, not just for local law enforcement but also for Stone and his family. Stone had returned to help his sister who was having health problems. Her symptoms of dizziness and nausea were intermittent and she needed his help running the resort. He had contacted law enforcement with plans of his return, and they had devised a plan that would hopefully force the perpetrator to make a move again and also clear him of any suspicion.

The local police had questioned him extensively after the first girl had been reported missing. Stone had been at the beach party the night of her disappearance, but so had probably 50 other young men and women. All the men at the party had been questioned. The missing person had been a local, heavily involved with other youth in the area. Many college students had come home for the summer, and the group of young men and women were often together evenings.

The disappearance of that young woman had become old news by the time he had been able to come home again. College studies, sports, and pretty women had kept him busy and away for a long time.

His sister Billie had been adamant that he come home for Easter all those years ago. He had returned, and, coincidentally, another young woman went missing. The police were at his sister Billie's door in short order.

"Where were you on the night of...who did you see...who saw you?" Interrogation had begun, and the hot seat was definitely sizzling.

Stone actually had an easily verified alibi, having been in church for a concert and later at the pastor's house for coffee. The missing woman had been at the concert also, and Stone had a short conversation with her during intermission. Again, many young people had been questioned, but no one had seen the woman disappear. Talk flew through the community, and anyone questioned was scrutinized by townspeople. There was considerable talk about Stone, the handsome rich son of the de'Buhr family. Speculation flew around like a witch looking for a place to land. Yes, he had an alibi, except for the time between church and the pastor's house and after he left there.

What was it, Stone would ask himself, that sparked the horrible phenomenon that he would, or could, cause people to vanish? Were they dead? Did they leave on their own? What happened to them? Did he know but not remember? Law enforcement agencies had questioned him so many times he had actually become friendly with them.

Stone and Billie's father ultimately died of a massive heart attack. Billie's husband, Jim, took over the resort, and their mother had continued to work there and watch the business thrive. Their mother died, and, shortly thereafter, Billie's daughter, Jennie, drowned. Before the year was over, Billie's husband had been killed in a freak car accident. Billie now had sole responsibility for running the resort.

Stone, Darryl, Brian, and Elliot had been friends since early in their youth. They all lived close to each other on Pokegama Lake and saw each other almost every day—swimming, boating, and fishing. Stone had to work at the resort, but that was almost like play much of the time. When the other boys were done with chores around their lake homes, they would come to the resort to help Stone.

The boys had actually enjoyed themselves. They raked the beach, cleaned the fire pits, and removed rocks from the pristine sugar sand that lay on the bottom of the lake. There was always trash to pick up around the cabins and beach. Part of their *work* was to fix S'mores, which were always a tasty treat. They would roast the marshmallows or help the youngsters hold the roasting sticks while the older children opened the graham crackers and Hershey bars. The boys were also infatuated with the girls—resort guests, whose parents rented cabins at Stonebridge for a week or month.

The four friends all played football. Brian, with his tall slight build, was wiry and had unbelievable strength in his arms. He was their school's unstoppable tight end. Elliot could run like a deer and added his quick moves to become a relentless running back. Darryl's hulky build and strength heralded him as a 'brick wall' linebacker. Stone was the Hidden Rapids Indians' spot-on quarterback. He could throw the ball high with great force and precision. Brian's height and remarkable agility enabled him to catch the ball far above the defender. Elliot's speed and agility to move and weave around the defenders like a ghost also contributed greatly to the Indians' many wins and trophies.

Brian and Elliot still lived in Hidden Rapids. Brian came back after college to take over his father's bank. Elliot, a doctor by training but now a mortician, had worked with his dad until his father passed away and he took over the business. Darryl left the state and worked as a broker. Stone had lost track of him until he heard the news of Darryl's death. He had attended the memorial service and had also met his cousin Cheryl. She was nice. Stone liked her well enough, but Brian had become so infatuated with her he had married her during a trip to Las Vegas.

Stone had been amazed at how much Cheryl and Darryl resembled each other. Of course Cheryl was more feminine, but she was still good-sized. Stone had thought they might even be double cousins. He had known two men who were double cousins: their mothers had married brothers, and the cousins looked remarkably alike. Brian and Cheryl had seemed happy and content the last time Stone saw them, so who could ask for more?

The four boys had become as close as brothers, and their friendships continued throughout their college years. Their closeness had diminished though: Darryl had died, and Stone's return visits had sparked the disappearance of women. Stone stopped coming home, although he and Billie had met at times when he had vacation or time off from his job as a pilot for the airlines. They would meet at a resort or motel somewhere not too far from Hidden Rapids or, occasionally, at a quaint resort in Wisconsin.

CHAPTER 7
"Every Day I Have to Cry Some"

———◆———

ROXANNE ROLLED OVER ON HER side and opened her eyes. As she gazed around the room, for just a second she wondered where she was. Then… ah, yes…this was her room—her life. She lay in bed for a few minutes, wondering how this all started, how and when it became so out of control. It felt as if it had happened overnight. Without warning a monster had taken over.

She placed her feet on the floor and put her slippers on. She quickly dressed, a rarity for her. She usually just stayed in her nightgown all day. Sometimes she would wear her yellow robe with the hem falling down if it were cold in the house. But today was different. Barry was coming to mow the grass and chances are they would have coffee together. There was just enough room for her to make her way to the kitchen. She could reach the coffee pot, and, with a good stretch, could fill it with water from the almost totally hidden sink. The faucet was so corroded it barely gave a trickle of water. As she looked out the window, she saw Barry unloading his lawn mower.

"Thank God for Barry," she said out loud as the animals running around her stopped, jerked, and barked. Seven dogs and 11 cats now huddled around her. They were hungry. She dug down into the bags for the dogs and cats. She saw a few bugs as she scooped, but she had learned long ago to disregard them.

Barry had kept her yard looking meticulously manicured for years. He had started taking care of it when he was in junior high. She smiled as she remembered how his working for her had started. He had come to her home to sell tickets to the class play. She had had a fond feeling for him for years. Barry's father, Jack, had been her first love. They may have even married had it not been for her parents. Jack was from a middle class family and they—the Abbotts—were definitely upper class.

Roxanne's parents had insisted she end her relationship with Jack. She had fought them for a while, but they were adamant that she and Jack's association end. They ultimately won that battle. Roxanne had always felt extremely close to her mom and dad and would never have done anything to alienate them.

Before long, another man, Charles, had come along. Handpicked by her parents, he was a genuinely good man, handsome, engaging, deep blue eyes, and an outgoing nature. She easily became interested in him, and they were married shortly after graduating college. Before long they had welcomed two children into their lives. Their son and daughter, Eric and Holly, were healthy and happy. Life was good.

Half walking, half sliding through a narrow pathway, she made her way to the family room where she usually watched the morning news. The papers stacked in front of the TV were too high to get a full view of the set. She knew she would have to deal with that one day...but not today.

A knock on the door startled her for just a second and set the dogs barking again for many minutes. She knew that signal. Barry was taking a coffee break and wanted her to join him.

This was her chance to hear about the outside world, and she savored the news Barry would bring her. His eyes were fixed on the side door where Roxanne would come out of her house. He grinned, waved, and shouted a friendly hello as he saw her coming out. She waved back.

Barry brought out his thermos and two large muffins: one blueberry, his favorite, and one banana nut, hers. Roxanne always brought her own cup. He told her the latest gossip, and he talked about his dad's lumberyard where he worked. He also brought her a church bulletin. Today his news was mostly about Billie.

Billie had been Roxanne's best friend before hoarding had taken over her life. Billie was ill and no cause had yet been found. Apparently she hadn't felt well for quite some time. Roxanne wished she could hop in her car and drive to Stonebridge to visit her old friend. She hadn't driven for so long; her car probably wouldn't start, or maybe she wouldn't even remember how to drive anymore.

Roxanne wondered sometimes what was said about her by the townspeople, what Billie had heard about her. A hoarder, she thought. It was mostly true if perhaps a little embellished. Her house was filled to overflowing with papers, magazines, books, clothes, and plenty of trash. She admitted she *was* a hoarder. How she hated that label. She supposed she hated that just like alcoholics and drug addicts hate their labels—even though that's what they were. She preferred to think of herself as a *collector.*

Physician, heal thyself, Roxanne would often think and wonder why she couldn't fix her own troubles—her craziness. She even thought she knew how it started. When her mom and dad were killed in a plane crash, her grief was inconsolable. She had cleaned out her parents' home and brought everything to hers, storing it all in a spare bedroom. It had become a shrine. She never moved or discarded anything in the *museum* she had set up for them. The dust grew thick, and the room even seemed to smell like death.

Charles and the children didn't seem to mind. The door to the storeroom, as it was now called, was usually closed, and no one except Roxanne ever went in there. Life went on. Eric graduated high school and joined the military. But news of his death in Afghanistan had sent Roxanne's already fragile mind into a tailspin. Eric's bedroom became the second museum in their home. Roxanne could part with nothing that had to do with him. His room, too, was soon piled high with memorabilia.

Household things, clothing, papers, and boxes cluttered the foyer. Before long the hallway to the living room could hardly be navigated. The stuff seemed to multiply by itself, appearing almost by magic.

Charles soon put his foot down, saying, "No more." Life would almost be normal, and then the collecting would start again.

Charles and their daughter had pleaded with her, threatened her, and even called Billie to come and help her friend. It was all for naught; her ogre was totally in charge.

One sunny fall morning, Charles, stumbling as he tried to negotiate his path out of the bedroom, threw up his hands, and said, "This is nuts. I'm all done with it." He packed a few things and left. Roxanne soon heard from his lawyer; their marriage was over. When the divorce papers arrived, she signed them without giving him any trouble.

Her daughter Holly was also quickly out the door; she lived with friends until graduation. Holly begged her mother to stop, but the hoarding just became worse.

Holly had eventually married her old friend Charlotte's son Josh, and now Roxanne had three children, two boys and a girl. They never came to the house, and that was how Roxanne wanted it. She had first visited Holly and Josh's home fairly often, bringing food from a restaurant and eating dinner with them at least once a week. However, that slowly became extremely difficult for Roxanne. Leaving the safety of her home and venturing out overwhelmed her, and the sense of being out of control was more than she could handle. She and Holly spoke on the phone occasionally, but it was awkward and forced. Neither of them knew how to cope with the dysfunction that now plagued Roxanne.

Roxanne loved springtime. Barry came over more often because the grass grew so fast it needed mowing every five days. He would bring a high school crew out to trim trees and clean out the flower gardens. Later, Bloomers Nursery would plant new window boxes, and Barry would bring them out. Roxanne was keenly aware that her yard and garden took a lot of Barry's time—time that he could be working at the lumberyard or spending with his family; but she paid him well, and he seemed to enjoy their visits as much as she did.

He never treated her as odd although she knew she was. Her degree in psychology should have helped her through her disorder. Thinking of it, she wondered if she could even find her diploma. She thought also of Billie—their years in college, even using their common educations to start their counseling practice. They had vowed to be friends until the day they died. Now here they were—not in any practice, not dead, and not friends. Well, maybe they were still friends; they just hadn't seen each other for a long time.

Billie had made several attempts to contact Roxanne. She had suggested they meet for lunch. "Come to Stonebridge for coffee. Sit in the sunroom with me or down on the beach." Billie's pleading had made Roxanne cry. She missed her dear friend but couldn't bring herself to venture out anymore; and the thought of anyone coming into her house was even more frightening.

Barry and Roxanne were soon finished with their coffee break. She hated to see it end. His visits were the highlight of her weeks. Now that spring was here, she would get to see him often.

Although the inside of her house could be described as a pigsty, her yard and flower gardens were beautiful. The yard looked like something out of Better Homes and Gardens. Barry knew to spare no expense when it came to the lawn and flowers. Roxanne was wealthy. She and her brother Brian had inherited their parents' sizable fortune. Roxanne's financial adviser had invested her inheritance wisely, and money was not a worry. Roxanne had long owned the peninsula that jutted out on the south side of Pokegama Lake just a few miles outside of Hidden Rapids. It had become extremely valuable. Many realtors and contractors had contacted her with offers to buy the gorgeous piece of property.

She and Brian had initially owned the land together for many years. Roxanne and Charles had built a fabulous house close to the shore before regulations were passed that now made being so close to the water illegal. Brian had put up a pole barn with intentions of building a house; but as the years passed, his wife, Cheryl, had wanted to live north of town in a secluded acre on Johnson Lake. He eventually sold all the property to Roxanne, only keeping a lifelong easement so he could have access to the pole barn.

Barry regularly mowed and trimmed around the pole barn even though Brian rarely used it. Roxanne would occasionally see light coming from it, and her dogs would alert her by barking and running to the window. She knew he still came there once in awhile.

Roxanne watched Barry load up his tools and lawnmower and drive down the lane. She was all alone again. Sitting in a high-back chair, she looked around the living room. The other furniture was hardly visible. In college she had read extensively about her illness—although it was not affecting her then. Feeling nervous and scared, she knew it often came with obsessive-compulsive behavior and perfectionism. Frequently, the mindset would be that if not able to do something perfectly, victims would do nothing at all. Roxanne understood that sometimes hoarders could lose their minds in the process of giving up their stuff.

She had extensively researched her illness, but her examination of the pertinent material did nothing to alleviate her fears. Roxanne knew it affected both men and women, no matter their age, and their income played little part in the affliction. The information also revealed that people who hoard often have unresolved trauma and loss in their lives. One loss too many often triggered syndromes that had been lurking in their behavior for years.

"Well, of course I have unresolved trauma and loss in my life," Roxanne said out loud to the dogs and cats that were now staring at her. "I've lost everything I ever loved."

Have I already lost my mind? she would ask herself at times, especially now that there were shows on television about hoarders. She had tried to watch one once but found herself so distraught she had to turn it off. She had cried for days after watching it for just a few minutes and could hardly lift her head off the pillow.

Roxanne believed if she were to throw something away, she would almost immediately need it. Her collections had become precious to her.

She prized them although they were mostly worthless in normal parlance. "These are mine—my possessions. This all belongs to me." She spoke the words out loud though only the animals in the house heard her.

Her *journey* this morning had gone well. It always felt like a long strenuous trek to leave the protection of her home and travel even the short distance to the picnic table on the porch. If it were not for Barry's coaxing a long time ago, she would have never left the prison she had created for herself.

Roxanne settled in for the great enjoyment of reading the church bulletin. Names of members were still so familiar. It may be their children now being confirmed or even married, but it gave her a sense of community, and she missed that. The pastor still called occasionally, asking if he could visit. She always said no; but she liked to imagine what it would be like to have him sitting in her living room, sipping hot tea together.

She had at one time been quite involved with the church. She had taught Sunday school and sang in the church choir. She had sung solos during church services, funerals, and weddings. Compliments about her beautiful voice had been many, and she had loved singing. What had happened to that pretty, self-assured woman?

Roxanne hadn't reminisced for a long time about the good days in her life. There had been many good days—actually good years. At first she smiled, remembering the wonderful times; but then her memories brought tears as she recalled the life she had once enjoyed. Again the questions: *When had the good times ended? How? And Why?*

CHAPTER 8

"I WILL REMEMBER YOU"

EMILY AWOKE IN THE SAME twin bed she had slept in for many years in her youth. When she was young, her weekends were almost always spent at the cabin. Summer brought swimming and boating; winter, ice skating, and snowmobiling. Feelings of peace and contentment filled her thoughts; she relished the morning. A hot cup of coffee on the deck and the scenery of the lake filled her heart with cherished memories. By mid-morning she had savored the sights along the lake.

With some free time on her hands, Emily decided to go to the cemetery. She had not seen her mother's grave in several years. It was close to the entrance, so she stopped there first. Recollections of a happy mother in her early childhood surfaced; she spent several minutes, pleasantly thinking about her mom and dad. They had laughed and affectionately teased each other, holding hands often when at sporting events or other community gatherings. There had been genuine love and passion for each other until gambling became more important than anything else in her life.

Emily brushed the grass from the recent mowing off her mother's marker.

Charlotte Blake
Born June 25, 1952
Died July 7, 1992

An attractive picture of her mother had been embedded in the marble headstone. Her mother's beautiful blue eyes seemed to look directly at her. *If only she could talk,* Emily thought tearfully. There had been so many things she would like to discuss with her. Emily's interior decorating business was going well. Her clients trusted her advice and liked her creativity and can-do attitude. That gift was from her mother who *could* turn a sow's ear into a silk purse.

She moved along, walking among the graves, and reading softly the names of the people buried in this quiet place. Emily slowly walked to Jenny's resting place. Jenny Westfield, the dearest friend in her life, had died when so young, so unexpectedly.

Emily crossed her legs and sat down on the grass. She ran her hand over the smooth gravestone and traced over the words etched in the black marble. The picture on the marker was of Jenny at a swim meet. Emily had been in that photo also but was cropped out; she could still see a bit of her own arm in the picture. They had just finished the state swim meet, Jenny taking first place and Emily, second.

A colorful angel wind chime gently played over the young girl's grave. Jenny had been laid to rest many years ago. The scene of her huge funeral flashed through Emily's mind. Disbelief had sent her into a daze that lasted for weeks. She could barely function, and her father had been at a loss of what to do. He had enlisted the help of a therapist; and Emily spent many sessions, trying to accept that Jenny was indeed dead. She had still felt Jenny's presence. It was as if her spirit had unfinished business and refused to leave the earth. Her body lay quiet and still, but her soul was not at peace. Jenny's cause of death had been ruled a drowning but unofficially was undetermined. Her spirit seemed to move around the graveyard restlessly.

Presently, Emily felt a cold hand brush across her face, startling her. Then a wispy figure of a woman in a gauzy white dress moved slowly along the edge of the graveyard. Frozen in fear, Emily could not make her legs move. When she finally could walk, she ran over to the last row of gravestones. The ghostly vision was gone. Terror filled her thoughts as she ran toward her car. Emily didn't believe in ghosts or spirits; but she also couldn't shake off the feeling of the cold hand that swept across her face nor the sight of the woman at the edge of the cemetery.

Emily saw a woman kneeling by a large black gravestone as she ran toward her car. Emily stopped, caught her breath, and spoke to her. "Did you see a lady in a white filmy dress by the edge of the graveyard?" she asked, frightened, almost breathless.

"No…," the lady answered with a puzzled look on her face. "I've only been here a few minutes and haven't seen anyone but you."

Emily quickly walked to her car, hopped in, and locked the doors. Trembling, she started the car and drove away. When she felt she had gone far enough to be safe, she stopped and buried her face in her hands. She cried from fear and sadness. She thought—no, she knew—it was Jenny. She knew Jenny had come to her—but why?

She thought of the dream, about the phone call, and the haunting voice of her dear friend. Emily knew enough about spirits and dreams of dead loved ones. She did not necessarily believe in ghosts but was open to the possibility of their coming back to this world, especially when there was unfinished business. She often dreamed of her mother—dreams that were pleasant, always about the good times, never the gambling and fights about the money her mother had lost. Emily was soon driving into the resort and trying to sort through what she saw…or at least what she thought she had seen.

Cheryl shook her head in wonderment at the face of the young woman who had just left the cemetery. The question about seeing anyone else and her disturbed expression left Cheryl feeling just a little creepy. She had come to the cemetery to mourn the loss of a person who now felt like a brother—almost—but not quite.

Perplexed by the young woman's ramblings, Cheryl now looked carefully around the entire cemetery. Seeing nothing and no one, she looked intently at the name engraved on the bronze colored marble stone.

Darryl Allen Schafer
Born September 9, 1972
Died April 20, 1997

Tears fell as she remembered the person whose memory was imprinted on the smooth shiny stone. She had loved him so much, but he had lived life with a mistake—a blunder that she had to make right—an error she had to correct. Regardless of his failings, she had loved him and now missed so many things about the man.

Darryl had been fearless and strong, determined and unstoppable. He had always felt sad but covered his feelings with an engaging smile and quick wit. His friends were many, and even adults couldn't help but like the youngster as he was growing up. He had been a high school and college jock, popular, and a good student. His days as a stockbroker were successful; and he had enjoyed his wealth and, subsequently, pleasurable material things. However, there was always something missing—always a feeling of not belonging—not feeling good in his own skin.

Cheryl's thoughts returned to the day of the visitation. She had spared no expense, and Elliot had provided a service fit for a king. After the wake, there had been hearty appetizers served at the Stonebridge Lodge and a moonlight ride on the cruise paddleboat provided by the resort. Slipping along the velvet lake, friends and relatives had memorialized Darryl. Stone, Elliot, and Brian each had stories to tell of their longtime friend. Laughter and tears had filled the evening.

The day of the memorial service, Immanuel Church had been filled with bouquets of flowers. The plants and cut flowers were so abundant that some lined the outer edge of the church pews. Darryl's body wasn't there, but an expensive bronze urn looked beautiful with flowers and candles surrounding it. Pictures of him were also plentiful, showing his life from birth to death. He was a man's man, a handsome hulk of a guy. He had never married, but there were many pictures of him with beautiful women.

A funeral without a body is so much easier. A small box sits there, letting a person imagine the ashes and pieces of bone inside. There is no last look at a loved one or friend, no touching the cold, stiff body, and no thought of the ground it will soon lie beneath.

Only two people knew what she had been through. Elliot watched her walk into the funeral home and had wondered about the woman who so closely resembled Darryl. "Is there actually a body?" he had asked, guessing that he already knew the answer. Brian had looked her over, looked hard at her the first time they met, and he knew—within a few minutes, he knew. Now on her knees, pulling the grass from around the stone and looking at the handsome picture staring at her, she sobbed. Emotions seemed to fill her thoughts and at some point would need to explode. Brian was understanding and comforted her— always sympathetic and doing his best to alleviate her fears and anxiety. Although it was love at first sight, he had also accepted that she still loved someone else.

They had made a good couple. Brian, an excellent businessman, had provided well for his loving wife. Cheryl had money of her own and, between the two of them, could finance anything they could possibly want. Cheryl knew the idiosyncrasy that plagued Brian and looked the other way. They had each come with baggage and understood the other. Cheryl often worried about Brian's safety. The Internet had become an anonymous place to act out his peculiarities, but it was also a place to arrange bizarre and dangerous meetings. Brian often placed himself in harm's way with strangers he was willing to meet in risky places. He always felt he was in control of the situations, but Cheryl knew better. She knew the perilous world of sex and degenerate behavior first hand. Her life had changed: she no longer engaged in deviant activities and was grateful to have come out alive from some of her own situations.

Brian was different. She at least had been worldly and physically strong. Brian was not muscular; and, although he imagined himself sexually sophisticated, he was not.

Cheryl sat on the grass by the gravesite, letting her thoughts return to their childhood days: ignorance and inexperience, but also unfailing confidence. Elliot, Stone, Darryl, and Brian had been inseparable friends. Theirs had been a life of magnificent adolescence. Their formative years had been spent on Pokegama Lake. Others envied the lives they enjoyed. The frosty months brought a winter wonderland of ice fishing and snowmobiling right outside their doors. Summer brought boating, swimming, water skiing, and fishing. She now had better control of her life and happiness, but she still lived with a secret—the secret that had long been denied, and, when she finally accepted herself, that she was still hiding.

CHAPTER 9

"TREAT ME LIKE A FOOL"

———◆———

AT 3:00 A.M. THE PHONE rang, abruptly waking Elliot out of a deep sleep. "Hello," he said groggily, trying to clear his throat.

The caller was distraught—common anytime but always when calling in the middle of the night. "It's the hospital," he whispered softly to his sleepy wife. "Louis has died."

Elliot was often awakened to take care of the deceased. People die every hour of the day, but most associate death, sadness, and trouble with the wee hours of the morning. No one expects a horrible accident during the day, although they occur as often then as any other time.

Louis Faulkner's wife was at the Hidden Rapids Hospital. Louis had fallen off his dock while trying to get into his boat. He had hit his head and had fallen into unconsciousness. She was now calling to tell Elliot that Louis had just died. His family was all at the hospital. Elliot said he would be there as quickly as possible.

Brittany had heard the phone but had not really awakened. She was used to the disruptive calls and not interested in getting up with Elliot.

Elliot's father had been a mortician, but Elliot had studied to be a surgeon. He had attended the University of Minnesota but had taken over his father's mortuary when his father died unexpectedly in his late 50s. They had worked together for years, and Elliot had gained experienced in the funeral business before actually taking the reins. The name Bennett was well known in northeastern Minnesota, with establishments in five localities. Four were not in large cities, but Duluth was a town of over 86,000, providing enough business to carry the smaller mortuaries.

Brittany had been raised in Duluth, and her family name was also quite well known. Their marriage had caused quite a stir—handsome Elliot Bennett marrying into the wealthy Cullen family. Shipping in the port city had made the Cullens millions.

Brittany was a snob, which didn't endear her to the rangers, loggers, and miners of Hidden Rapids. She had intended to marry a doctor and live a more exciting life. Perhaps he would start a practice in California where she would socialize with movie stars, or in the east, where she would mingle with politicians. She had not envisioned staying in northern Minnesota. There was certainly no one there she considered her equal. Brittany had been furious when Elliot told of his decision to stay in Hidden Rapids to be a funeral director. He would also take over the job of coroner. He tried to explain his change of heart, choosing to care for the dead as a mortician over improving the health of the living as a surgeon.

"But you're already a doctor," she had screamed with a clenched fist. "You can't just stop and be a mortician. I would never have married you if you weren't going to be a medical practitioner...away from this humdrum existence."

"That was my mother's dream," he would say with a tone of regret. To a degree, he felt sorry about walking away from the medical profession, but he had never really felt the calling, though he used his anatomical expertise.

Brittany knew about the fall and the precarious situation Louis was in. It didn't surprise her. She mumbled something like 'sorry' and fell back to sleep. Elliot watched her lying there as he pulled on his pants and grabbed his shirt, still watching Brittany slowly breathing, lying nude in their king size bed. She was gorgeous. Her long auburn hair lay lightly along the side of her face. Her lips perfectly formed after a visit to the plastic surgeon had a pouty look even as she slept. He longed for the days when they had truly been a happily married couple. They had loved each other with unstoppable passion. He grinned as he thought back on their days of lust and love. He had been able to control his demons then, keeping them only as fantasies and never acting on them.

Elliot and Brittany seemed to connect the moment they met. Their wants and dreams were the same, and compatibility seemed to be what forged their close feelings for each other. He had wanted to get out of his home area as much as she had. However, Elliot's unnatural urges had increased each year. His longtime friend Brian thought it was their involvement with what many of the townspeople had called a cult—Satan's family. A full moon swept through Elliot's—and Brian's—psyches like an electrical storm, unleashing fervor they could not contain. April 15, 2014, October 8, 2014, and most recently April 4, 2015, when the Blood Moon rose, their raging lunacy gripped them like a vise. They had no control, which was both frightening and exhilarating. The moon would turn to blood again on the 28th of September, and Elliot was waiting for the next madness to appear.

As their marriage turned into a struggle, with love on the back burner and the clash of wills constantly on the front, Elliot reverted to the world of the dead. The full moon took control of his willpower, and the urges that he had kept under control became more powerful. He felt comfortable around the dead: They were his company—his friends. He had known his bizarre urges were strange, but that had been a long time ago, and they seemed perfectly normal now. Brittany's constant, emasculating criticism over the years had forced him to seek other ways to soothe his body and mind.

Elliot and his best friend Brian straddled life between normal and bizarre. They were upstanding men in the community, always ready to raise funds for projects or willing to put a strong back into hard physical work for the betterment of Hidden Rapids. But they could also march to a very different drummer when the dark sky filled with the light of a full moon. The blood moons that had come last year in the early spring and again in October had brought their abnormal behavior to new heights. Again this year in early April, their minds had come close to exploding. A curious woman would leave home—laundry, unfolded; bills, not paid; missing the parent-teacher conference the next afternoon. Their unnatural activities had begun to frighten even them.

Elliot drove to the Itasca County Hospital with memories tumbling through his mind. He longed for his younger days. He had loved high school sports and the adulation he and friends Darryl, Stone, and Brian had experienced. He yearned for those carefree, endless summer days filled with swimming, boating, picnics, and dates with pretty young girls.

The parking lot at the hospital was almost empty; but, then, it was early morning. The new area hospital was state of the art and an invaluable asset to the community. Elliot was instrumental in getting the financing for the impressive medical complex. He considered himself, and Brian also, to be intricate parts of this community. Their involvement in the fundraising needed to get the project started made them indispensable.

Louis's doctor greeted Elliot. His grieving widow and children sat in the lounge next to the nurses' station. Elliot put on his professional face and hugged Mrs. Faulkner. He filled out paper work at the desk and then walked out the door and loaded the corpse.

Brian and he were still very close and saw each other several times a week. They met at the Beachcomber for dinner on a regular basis. Their wives did not care for each other, so that was actually fine with them. They liked being together without their wives. Brittany spent most of her time correcting Elliot on every subject he and Brian talked about. Brittany acted like she knew everything about any subject that might come up, and she certainly knew that Elliot had the facts about almost anything wrong. Cheryl just rolled her eyes and took deep breaths if she had to be subjected to Brittany. Cheryl enjoyed being with the men but not if Brittany were included.

The men met for coffee also. Mornings would find them at Cheech's Café in downtown Hidden Rapids. They would sit at the counter so as not to take up a table if they intended to stay awhile. A librarian, a pharmacist from the drugstore next door, an auto mechanic, and a woman who worked at Anderson Lumber often sat along side them. They would solve all the problems of the world before coffee and rolls were finished.

CHAPTER 10

"YOU ALWAYS HURT THE ONE YOU LOVE"

———◆———

EMILY AWOKE ON THIS BRIGHT and sunny day and knew it was the day to visit her father. They had been close; however, her move to California did not please him, and they had drifted apart. They still talked, though not regularly; but, whenever something to do with the cabin or other financial decisions came up, he would call, having named her as personal representative with power of attorney.

Northern Exposure Assisted Living looked inviting. The large structure had been perfectly planned to fit in the north woods. Resembling a sprawling log house with warm subdued lighting and soft earthy colors, it embraced the tranquility of the surrounding landscape. There were lavish apartments with views of the lake and dense forest; the air smelled of pine and water. The complex had been built with an inheritance from a wealthy logger, but all residents, rich or poor, were welcome. There was also an Alzheimer's unit and full-care nursing home.

Emily's father had been rehabilitated after his stroke and able to live in one of the apartments. Emily knew that Lucy Fox, his long-time secretary at the lumber yard, lived in the apartment across the hall and that they were together most of the day, perhaps the night also. Emily knew that, if not for her occasional visits to her father, they would probably live together, perhaps even marry. Emily had never been comfortable with Lucy and her father's relationship. Even after her mother's death, she didn't like to see Lucy Fox and her dad together. There was something unsettling about her.

Lucy and Emily's father had been lovers for years. The whole town knew but didn't seem to care. Her mother's gambling addiction had taken their family finances from boom to bust many times. When her mom died, life had become calm and more predictable. That sense of impending doom that had hovered over their lives disappeared, and Paul Blake had smiled again. That hadn't lasted long because a debilitating stroke hit him at middle age. Forced to sell his half of the lumber business, he now moved around slowly. He had made good progress the last years, and Emily would hear occasionally from her dad and Lucy. She wished she could like Lucy. There were many good things about her—if Emily could just get past the long-time affair she had had with her dad. Her mother had been a gambler and probably a lousy wife and mother; but she was her mother, and Emily had loved her.

Emily hugged her father, sat next to him, and held his hand. She was pleased that he no longer needed a wheelchair. When tears welled in his eyes, she cried with him: tears of remorse for her but tears of happiness for him. Paul had longed for his family to be physically close to him and emotionally attached as well; but family ties had been severed, and he didn't know why.

Josh lived in the area but had been estranged for so long; and Paul believed Emily had fled the scenic northern woods she had loved without an explanation. When asked for a reason, she had made a flippant remark about finding herself. "Are you lost?" he had asked with equal sarcasm. He had apologized the moment the words flew from his month. Paul Blake was not a smart aleck. Emily knew that, but nothing could change her decision to leave.

Lucy had been in Paul's apartment when Emily arrived but graciously greeted Emily, excused herself, and left. Paul brought out albums, and they spent hours going through pictures. Laughing and crying as they paged through years of memories, they saw day give way to night. Emily joined her father for dinner.

Northern Exposure was high-class senior living. The dining room had large round tables covered with white linens, and the walls were filled with trophies. Glass-eyed deer, moose, wolves, and coyotes stared at the people drinking wine with their dinners of Chicken Kiev, wild rice, and mixed vegetables. Dessert was apple or cherry pie served with ice cream and coffee. Lucy had joined them at their table.

"I'm not going to stay in Hidden Rapids long, Dad," Emily said, looking for a reaction from her father.

To Emily's surprise, it was Lucy who responded. "I think that's best dear. No need to stay around and stir things up."

Emily was dumbfounded by Lucy's statement and couldn't stop herself from snapping off a curt, irritated reply. "Why would you say that?" and "What business is it of yours anyway?" The angry words floated around, and the room was suddenly quiet. The look on Paul's face showed dismay and hurt. Emily had embarrassed herself and her dad. Lucy left the table.

"Sorry dad, but what was that even all about? What does she think I am going to stir up?"

"I don't know, Honey"

His term of endearment went straight to her heart. It had been so long since he had called her Honey. She unexpectedly felt like a child again, got up from the table, and gave him a hug.

"I'll call you later," she said in a soft humiliated voice, knowing they would all three be the talk of the complex for many days to come.

Emily felt ashamed of her behavior as she made her way to the car. Her explosive words had been impossible to suppress. She had not felt such anger in years. Lucy's words kept coming back as she made her way to the cabin. *Stir up? What in the world had that meant? What on earth would I stir up?*

Lucy left the dining room as quickly as she could get up from her chair and walk out. She went back to her apartment and sank into her recliner. She would take back the words she had just uttered if she could. The words—like the smoke from a spent bullet—had hung in the air and filled the room. She had loved Paul for so many years and would never have hurt him or his children in any way.

Getting ready for bed, Lucy thought of her young life. Brushing her hair out of the tight bun, she looked in the mirror. The years had been gentle with her, and she did not look as old as she felt right now. Washing her face took some of her anxiety away, and she thought of Paul, that she and Paul should have been married when they were young. They would have had a happy life if it hadn't been for Charlotte, who had sucked the life out of Paul and the children financially and emotionally. She had finally died; but by that time, the children's contempt for Lucy was so strong that there was no getting over it.

Lucy had started to work for Paul as soon as she finished her vocational secretarial course. He needed a secretary and bookkeeper, and she needed a job. He had treated her with such respect and kindness; and she fell in love with him and the lumber business. Their affair hadn't started for years, although Lucy had been infatuated with Paul from their first meeting.

Scenes of long ago ran through her brain like a horror movie. Shortness of breath and cold perspiration followed her memories as she questioned who she had been all those years ago. Wondering how she had gotten involved with that religion—that fanatic. There had been so many followers who had been mesmerized by him. No one thought it was a cult. Even the word now, as she said it in a whisper, the thought of having been caught up in the craziness, did not seem real. It had taken place in a different life—at a different time. She had just left home, having saved enough money working in the summer to afford community college. She was excited when she got a job at the lumberyard.

Hidden Rapids had seemed like a large city compared with the little town she had grown up in. It felt good to get off the Range, and Lucy had never felt homesick. Home hadn't been much of a place—not just because the house was old, but the word *home* didn't really fit the drinking and fighting she had witnessed for as long as she could remember.

Leaving home had been an escape for her, and falling into the quagmire of that fanatical cult was a terrible mistake. At first, it had been a place of friendship, love, and understanding. Lucy had felt accepted, wanted, and important. It had evolved slowly, being more sinister than anyone could have ever imagined.

She had heard the rumors from Paul. They shared everything—well almost. He had told her about the police's belief that Emily and Josh actually knew something about Jenny's death—her drowning—if in fact it had been a drowning. "Perhaps," he had even told her in a sad sounding voice, "perhaps she had been murdered." It had hurt to hear those words, wondering if they may have seen Jenny in those last moments? "Well I can't live my life over," she said out loud, then turned down the covers and crawled in.

Sleep was a long time in coming as her thoughts journeyed to her youthful days. Her involvement with the religious cult was at that time in her life overwhelming, choking the moral compass right out of her. It had been replaced by the will of the Ruler. Lucy had left that life and gone on with a settled existence. She severed her relationship with the cult when they sacrificed what they considered to be *the lamb*. The woman she had become was no more. Memories of that awful time—that lapse of reason—seemed to have been a nightmare. It had to have been. Lucy knew she was a good person—and knew in her own heart that she would never be involved with anything criminal.

She wished Emily had stayed away. Emily's estrangement from her brother Josh and the uneasiness she had with her father had served Lucy well. She and Paul loved each other, and these last years, lived as husband and wife, usually in Paul's apartment, although Lucy kept hers also.

The words from Joel 2:31, "The sun shall be turned into darkness, and the moon into blood," haunted her thoughts.

CHAPTER 11

"Zip-a-Dee-Do-Dah"

———◆———

"TODAY'S THE DAY," BARRY TOLD his wife Debbie with a big grin on his face.

"Why today?" she asked, standing behind him, massaging his shoulders.

"Cuz I feel good about the outcome. I feel lucky today." He turned around and gave her a kiss and a hard hug. He had worked long and hard on the proposal. Now he needed Brian's go-ahead to talk to Roxanne. Barry was quite sure that Roxanne was the owner of the property, but Barry believed she might need her brother Brian's permission to sell. The lakeshore he wanted was pristine and had been coveted by many in the construction and realty business. He had asked himself all the questions that he thought would be pertinent, and Barry had an answer for all of them.

As soon as there was a break in customer traffic coming into the lumberyard, Barry walked across the street and down a block to the bank. Brian was helping a man with a car loan but soon finished and motioned Barry to come into his office.

Barry sat down in a comfortable black leather chair. Brian greeted him with a smile and a handshake. Barry declined the offer of coffee, instead laid out his proposal on the bank president's desk. Brian's cordial manner changed when he became aware of the property Barry wanted to buy.

"It's not for sale. That property will *never* be for sale." Brian's voice had started off at a normal pitch but now reached a loud almost booming decimal. He was on his feet, pushing his desk away from himself and into Barry's stomach. Rage filled his eyes. Barry, unnerved, tried to slip out of the chair but was pinned between the chair and desk. Brian's secretary heard the commotion and hurried into the office to ask what was wrong. Her tone and presence calmed the bank president, and, before long, Brian wiped his sweaty red face and apologized to Barry.

Brian was still adamant that the property was not for sale; and so the meeting ended, his rage smoldering. He explained that the property had been in the family for many years, that it was special to him and to his sister, and that she would never want to sell. He went on to say that even approaching her about the subject would upset her already fragile mental state. Trying hard to maintain his composure, he shook Barry's hand and said they had nothing further to discuss.

Barry walked into his dad's office at the lumber yard, slumped into a chair, and said, "Brian Abbott is nuts."

His dad looked puzzled and commented that there was something different about Brian, but no one was exactly sure what it was. He could be a bit peculiar, maybe even creepy at times; but it had always been a hard thing to put a finger on. He was just a bit of an odd duck.

"I want that property, Dad. Paulson Construction and I have worked out a deal. It would be a win-win for everyone, and even Roxanne would be happy. None of the homes would be built close to her. She would still have her privacy; and, although she doesn't need the money, she doesn't need all that lake shore either." Barry was worked up and angry.

"Just go to Roxanne," Jack said. "She doesn't need his permission to sell. It all belongs to her except that little piece of land that his pole barn sits on—and that's inconsequential. Go right to her, lay out your proposal, and let her think it over. She likes you and I think will trust you. Just make sure you are honest and forthright. Answer all her questions, and reassure her that her life would not be disrupted. That's the truth, isn't it: Her life would not be upset?" Jack wanted his son to be able to pursue this endeavor but also had a soft spot for Roxanne. Her life had been chaotic enough without his son adding to it. Roxanne was a fragile woman, and he wanted her delicate condition to be considered while dealing with her.

The next morning, Barry gathered his building proposal and stopped at the bakery for the usual muffins. He loaded his lawn mower and weed whip into the back of his pickup and prayed that Roxanne would, at the very least, listen to what he had to say. He worried about the rail-thin woman with sunken eyes. She was getting into her 60s, and her health would eventually be an issue. Who would care for her was a question he had asked himself. The woman for whom he had mowed, trimmed, and planted flowers had no one to call on for help. He understood her daughter Holly's disgust. Roxanne's hoarding was understandably exasperating; but it was a disease—a horrible sickness that had consumed her every minute of every day for years.

Barry did his usual mowing in two hours. Then, taking a break, he knocked on the door to let her know he was ready for their coffee break. She quickly joined him with a friendly smile of welcome on her face.

Barry poured them each a cup of coffee and brought out the folder. As he opened it, he told Roxanne of the sale and construction plans he proposed. She sat still, looking almost spellbound. Barry carefully told her of each step, selling just one lot at a time. Barry would buy the first lot from her. Paulson Construction would build a spec house on the lot. Once that house sold, they would use the proceeds to buy another lot and build another home to sell. If at any time Roxanne changed her mind, the contract would end, and she could keep the rest of the property.

Neither spoke for what seemed like many minutes but was in truth maybe one or two. Barry, feeling compelled to give her every ounce of information she should have, told her of his visit with Brian and Brian's emphatic refusal to consider the sale of any of the land.

Roxanne was gracious, finishing her coffee, thanking Barry for his visit, and telling him that she would consider his offer and let him know. She was polite and cordial, but Barry could not get a sense of her real feelings. Roxanne's consideration of his proposal was all Barry had hoped for. He was left feeling his pitch at least stood a chance.

Roxanne returned to her house; Barry finished the yard work. She cleared a spot on the kitchen counter where her desk had once been and cleaned off the mostly buried desk chair. She sat down on the chair and moved her hand slowly across the newly cleaned area. Running her hand over the counter felt good. She grinned, seeing a small section of the beautiful gold and brown granite and feeling its smoothness. It had been so long but the beauty was still there.

Roxanne took a deep breath and really looked around her kitchen. She couldn't cook anymore. The stovetop was covered with papers and magazines. She wondered why the stove was such a mess. Memories of an immaculate kitchen were still there for she had once kept a clean house, a neat home.

She opened the folder and read the proposal. There wasn't a more beautiful spot on the lake, and her family had owned it for years. The fact that Brian had been so insistent that the land not be sold made her angry. It wasn't his call. She and Brian had never been close, but they used to see each other, at least occasionally. She wasn't sure exactly when that had ended, but it had been a long time, so this proposal was none of his business.

Roxanne read and reread the offer. She trusted him and his father, Jack. Her thoughts went back to her high school days. She and Jack had fallen in love. It couldn't have been too strong, she told herself, or they would have been together to this day. Her parents' influence and determination to break them up was stronger than anything they could hang on to, but Jack had most certainly been her first love. She knew how powerful that feeling could be for she was a voracious reader, books being one part of her house full of things she couldn't part with. In many of those books, reference was made to a first love, an enduring love that was never forgotten.

She wondered for just a moment what would have happened if she had rebelled against her parents, that is, if she refused to give Jack up. A grin spread across her face as she imagined the look her mother would have had—a look of total bewilderment. Roxanne never fought with her parents or went against their wishes. They had controlled her life, but she had also loved them. Their sudden deaths had been so devastating she still could not bring herself to visit their graves. She had not been there since the day of their funeral.

Roxanne had needed medication to help her through that time. Their funeral was a foggy memory, and the days and weeks following it were still only hazy thoughts. Brian had handled all the details. Roxanne had gone to the funeral home to plan the funeral but had become so physically ill, throwing up so violently, that the doctor had to be called. Roxanne could not even stay long enough to choose the songs to be sung. At the service, the sight of the caskets in the funeral home had sent her flailing on the floor. Her husband took her to the car and, after the service, back home.

Her mind was racing. What if she sold some of this property to a de-veloper? What would become of the quiet privacy she enjoyed? Enjoyed? No: Needed! She had a phobia about having too many people around her. She didn't even know when it had started. There had been a time when she was quite involved in the community—a member of many or-ganizations and even in charge of a few. She had loved to be around people, actually loving company.

But all that had changed. She continued to sit on her desk chair. The chair she hadn't sat in for so long felt like an old friend—a long lost friend. Roxanne began to trace her descent into hoarding, the disorder that had imprisoned her and had pulled her into an abyss she couldn't escape. Her parents' deaths certainly impacted her, but was her mental state that frail? Was she so void of coping skills she couldn't pull herself away from the illness's torturing grip?

She stood up and walked out of the kitchen, vowing to keep that space, that small, smooth gap on her counter, clean.

CHAPTER 12

"No Surrender"

———◆———

ROXANNE AWOKE TO THE SOUND of barking dogs and a slamming car door. Looking out her window, she could see that a car was indeed in her driveway. Fear rushed through her for just a moment, and then she realized that it was her brother Brian. She hadn't seen him in so long and wasn't excited with his presence in her space. She stumbled, trying to hurry to the door, slipping on the newspapers and magazines that were stacked in high, disheveled piles on the floor. Half walking, half sliding, she finally made it to the door. With her dogs and cats surrounding her, she opened the door, shielding the visitor from her animals.

"I've got to talk to you," Brian said urgently. Roxanne slipped out the door and stood in the porch with just her nightgown on. She was embarrassed, but Brian didn't seem to notice how she was dressed.

"Barry wants to buy the property on the lake. He can't, and you need to tell him in no uncertain terms that you absolutely will not sell—not now, not ever," he said angrily, his voice quivering, his face showing panic.

"Calm down, Brian. I haven't decided what I will do just yet," Roxanne said smugly. "I promised I would give the proposal my utmost consideration and let him know my decision in a week," she said, enjoying a long-lost sense of power.

"I can't believe you are even *thinking* about selling any of this beautiful lakeshore—our parents' lakeshore, the family cemetery." Brian was sweating now and fuming at the mere thought of anyone else living on the peninsula.

"It's not our parents' lakeshore Brian—not yours either—it's mine. It all belongs to me. You will still have your easement to the pole barn, and the family cemetery will always have an easement so we can visit it and have access to it for our own burials if that's what we want," Roxanne said. She had hit her stride. She owned the property and had the right to decide what to do with it.

"You can't sell it! I forbid it! I absolutely forbid it!" he shouted, saliva spraying from his mouth.

Roxanne was speechless for a moment, unnerved by Brian's wild behavior. She had never seen him act like this. He had always been such a gentle sort—a bit odd at times but never aggressive.

She took a deep breath and said as slowly and calmly as she could that he would have to leave.

He stormed off toward the car, still screaming that she had better not sell or she'd be sorry.

Disturbed by her meeting, she played it all again in her mind as she settled into her living room chair. What in the world could have upset him so much? He had never had a soft spot for this land and lakeshore. *She* had been the one who had loved the gorgeous peninsula. He never visited the family cemetery. Neither did she, for that matter, but they would always own a part of the property so they would have a way in to the burial plots.

As she relived the talk with Brian, she had to give herself credit. Roxanne hadn't interacted with anyone except Barry in a long time. She hadn't talked with Brian in years, and even then, they had certainly not had a confrontational conversation. Roxanne held her own today; she had forgotten her own issues and stood her ground. She felt proud of herself. She sat down to catch the evening news, feeling suddenly in control. She hadn't felt like that in so long, and it was intoxicating.

Roxanne closed her eyes and thought of the peaceful secluded family cemetery that was out of sight but not too far from her home. She had often gone there as a child. Her grandparents were buried there, as were many relatives born in the late 1800s and early 1900s. Two young children, buried together in one grave, had died in a house fire. Two older brothers from the same family had each died the same day from scarlet fever. They must have grieved for years, she thought, but eventually, the little family graveyard became a place of remembrance and peace…at least until her parents died and later her son. Now it was a depressing place, and Roxanne hadn't been there since the day her parents died, not even when Eric was interred. She had fainted that cold December afternoon as she watched his casket being slid into the back of the hearse. The burial took place without her.

Roxanne had long known she had unfinished business, but she was never quite sure if it was something simple or if it was more complex. Though the hoarding issue was complicated enough, she also knew it took guts to get better. Her life now was at least predictable. Fear of the unknown kept her in the prison of her home. It was hard to believe she was actually comfortable in this garbage dump, but she was. She felt safe here.

Yet she missed being able to see her dear friend, Billie, and her daughter, Holly, and grandchildren. Why couldn't she give up all this stuff? Tears flowed as she looked around her home. Just the word *home* no longer fit her state of affairs. This was no longer a home. It was a run-down shack that had, at one time, been a source of great joy.

Her parents had given Roxanne and Charles a sizeable chunk of property on Pokegama Lake as a wedding gift. Charles had soon drawn the plans for their house. It was now 30 years old but, for the last years, had certainly not been cared for. She dreamed of a place that would really fit the word *home* again. But that would mean giving up her stuff, her animals, and her privacy.

Sitting by the window, watching people race jet skis across the lake, she felt slightly envious. Skiing behind her family's boat was once exhilarating and addictive. She could ski for hours, never tiring, always ready for more water activities. Memories of the aroma of meat cooking on the grill and nighttime fires in their large fire pit forced a wide grin onto her face. She did not think of those wonderful days often because she was too busy, trying to manage her illness and struggling to get through the day.

Roxanne was in the mood for reminiscing. She closed her eyes and thought of her friends Billie and Charlotte. The three of them had been stars on the swim team. Thinking of swimming, her memories went to Jenny, Billie's daughter, whose life was taken by the one love they all had—beautiful Pokegama Lake. Jenny had been as good a swimmer as her mother. How she could have drowned would forever be a mystery.

Roxanne was still well at that time and able to help Billie through the quagmire of sorrow. They had sat for hours on the porch of Stonebridge Resort. Sometimes they cried together; other times, they were quiet—silence being the comfort Billie needed. Days went by and then weeks. Finally Billie had felt ready to run the resort again, and her need for Roxanne to be there with her all the time subsided.

Roxanne again reached for the proposal Barry had brought to her. The small clean area on her counter became more appealing every time she touched it. Just the feel of it made her happy. Reading and rereading the file seemed to transform her from being frightened of life in general into a strong powerful woman. She took great pains in carefully looking at the plans for the first spec house. It was a three-bedroom design, all on one floor with no basement. The master bedroom and bath were on one side of the house; an open living room, dining room, and kitchen were in the middle; the other two bedrooms and bath were on the opposite side. It was a simple but livable design. A large deck overlooked the lake, and the two-story boathouse had a one-bedroom guest apartment above.

Roxanne liked the plan. It looked as if it flowed with ease and would be affordable, although anything with lakeshore frontage was, from the beginning, expensive. The lot was a goodly distance from Roxanne's, possibly to give her a chance to get used to people living in her *space*. Even clearing some of the trees would not make the new house visible from hers. A grove of trees would still give her privacy.

She had told Barry she needed a week, and that time was going quickly. Her stomach churned as she thought of house plans and people on her stretch of beach. There was plenty of room for others in the actual scheme of things, but she had become so reclusive the thought of even seeing anyone close up made her fearful.

Reflecting again, she asked herself questions out loud. The first was, "What are you actually so frightened about—what scares you about seeing people?" Thoughts ran quickly through her head about how odd people thought she was, how they had stared at her when she first began hoarding. It had, of course, started slowly with her parents' things and then her son's possessions. She had felt closer to them with their belongings around her. She hadn't even noticed she was spending more time at home and less time doing the things she used to love. Charles would ask why she wasn't going to functions in town or out with the girls for lunch. Usually sociable, Roxanne had stopped having her weekly dinner parties and also felt her love of the outdoors subside.

"Could I ever get my life back? The life I used to have?" She spoke to her oldest and most loved of all her dogs. Duke had been a stray when she found him lying on the beach by her boatlift. His left leg had been injured. She had brought him to the vet and had also advertised the stray dog in the lost-and-found section of the weekly Hidden Rapids newspaper. When no one responded, she adopted him as her own. The Springer Spaniel puppy was soon a part of the family. Roxanne had collected other stray dogs and many cats that came her way, but none was as special as Duke.

This is the first time she had thought of a different life in a very long time. Her life today was usual, predictable, and safe. She had learned how to handle the day-to-day problems and worries in her life. Occasionally she would catch herself, worrying about getting older, about needing a doctor, or help getting around. She knew there was no one who would come to work for her inside her home; neither could she stand the thought of anyone else coming into her comfort zone—that is, her mess.

She would eventually need someone to help her, and unless she changed her ways, it was not going to be her daughter Holly. What if she became horribly ill or fell and needed to go to the hospital? The thought of calling 9–1–1, of needing an ambulance, or even having to enter a doctor's office made her sick to her stomach with fear.

CHAPTER 13

"SWEET DESIRE CARRIED ME AWAY"

———◆———

SEXYMAN4U SCROLLED THROUGH CRAIG'S LIST and clicked on the *personals* tab. There Brian found all types of men and women who were looking for a variety of sexual desires and fetishes. This was so much easier than it had been years ago. Women and men were now easy to contact, the computer affording so much anonymity.

He looked fondly at the array of fingernail polish he had collected. When he was young, he had stolen bright colors from drug stores. Later, he would buy them at the grocery store, being careful to include a few other feminine products so the checkout clerk would think the items were for his wife or girlfriend. The purchases were always made in Duluth, far enough away for him to remain unknown. Now, he simply went through the self-checkout lines at local stores, anonymously of course. Living out his fantasies had become so easy for him. His marriage to Cheryl had also made his unusual taste in sexual desires so much simpler.

Cheryl's face came to mind. Just the thought of her made him happy. How he was so lucky to find a person who would accept his quirky thoughts was nothing short of a miracle. She understood him; they understood each other. They knew the secrets that plagued their lives; they both liked walking on the wild, crazy side. Brian was actually shy and quiet until he was in a particular mood—a mood that didn't come often, but, when it did, he needed to act and act on it quickly. He needed relief from his mania. As he aged, the obsessions didn't come as often and weren't as powerful as they had once been, nor had the trigger been as available as it had been many years ago. The power was still there; but the circumstances of his bizarre acts were fewer, and chances to act on them were more dangerous. The police had become more savvy than ever—and suspicious. DNA testing had become a reliable science, and great care had to be taken not to leave a trace of anything behind.

He was excited about his new purchases. "Good Golly, Miss Trolley," "Keeping Suzi at Bay," "This Little Piggy," and "There's No Escaping" were just a few of the new colors in nail polish this summer, and he was energized, ready to make use of them. He needed someone to try them on, and meeting that special someone was getting finalized. The web provided privacy but an array of conquests, too. Or at least that was his thinking.

2_hot_for_u_Jessie had responded to his request for an open-minded woman who was eager to try new things, anything that gave sexual pleasure. He would meet her at Sugar Lake. She was a little skeptical of meeting outdoors, but he had assured her that it would be exciting and safe. There would be privacy at his trysting site with all the comforts of a quiet motel. He loved the seclusion of the beautiful area. It wasn't far from home, and its isolation was romantic. Brian needed his encounter with women to be adventurous, daring, and, with Stone back in the area, absolutely private.

When Cheryl came home, Brian had told her about the conversation with Barry. "He could cause all k- k- k- kinds of trouble if he were allowed to go ahead with this." He stuttered a little when he got excited. "I went to Roxanne's and demanded that she say no."

Cheryl had just walked in the door after a long day of hard work and was caught off guard. Brian was rarely this agitated, and she was taken aback by his drama. "Take it easy, buddy," she said light-heartedly, giving him a thump on his back. "She can't sell without your okay, can she?"

"Yes, she can," Brian said, his eyes reflecting his fear. "I signed that property over to her so she would have to pay all those high lakeshore taxes. All I have is an easement to get to my pole barn and the land it sits on."

"Oh, settle down." Cheryl soothed him with a softer voice and began rubbing his back. "We won't let her sell. We'll talk to her again and reason with her." Cheryl's voice was reassuring. Brian knew his wife could handle anything.

When Cheryl had stepped into his life many years ago, she had saved him from the vortex that would most certainly have killed him. She had calmed his wounded spirit and helped him manage his fetishes. His obsessions had become so strong he was no longer able to predict his reactions to anything.

Brian would again try talking Roxanne out of selling before Cheryl would get involved. Roxanne had thought Cheryl to be quite strange and expressed her dislike for Brian's choice of a wife.

"She's peculiar," Roxanne had said after meeting her. "Different—very unusual—something is disturbing and yet familiar about her." Roxanne had rolled her eyes and lifted her eyebrows as she spoke all those years ago.

Brian and Roxanne had never been close, so over time they had drifted ever farther apart with hardly a notice from either of them. Roxanne had drifted into the abyss of hoarding; and his problems kept him just one step ahead of lunacy, so his ability to help anyone was nil.

Brian had big plans for tonight and would not let Roxanne or her thoughts of selling lake property interfere with his fantasy. The rendezvous would take place on Sugar Lake. Thick woods gave way to a small clearing on the aqua colored water and provided a private quiet place for the kind of intimate meeting Brian had planned. A businessman from Minnetonka owned the lakeshore and rarely came to his cabin. Brian knew when the owner would be coming, as he and Brian always met for a drink when he arrived for the weekend.

The dark green tent was easy to set up. It quickly became a perfect place for a romantic date. Battery operated candles and fragrant potpourri lent an ambiance of pleasure. He wouldn't have to court the person coming for an evening of enjoyment, but he still liked the pleasantries of getting to know each other. It was of course superficial but very much a part of his fantasy. He also planned to manicure her nails and lined his choices of colors along the small white table covered with a leopard-print cloth. He had carefully chosen the bottles of polish not only for their colors but also for their names, which added to his fantasy. Gratification would be what they were each looking for; however, he liked to entice the woman into more of a lover's role than just a sex partner.

The disappearing sun glistened on the crisp blue water as a car pulled into the peaceful surroundings. Eagles circled the water, looking for prey. His had just arrived.

Jessie emerged from the elegant silver Cadillac. She was a real beauty. Sporting a red jacket, a white lace blouse, red leather leggings, black boots and a wide toothy smile, she waved to Brian. Long silver and black earrings dangled to her shoulders, and her eyes sparkled with silver eye shadow and black mascara. Jessie was truly delightful to the eye. Brian had met many women and an occasional man from the sex sites on the Internet—some pathetic, some mediocre, but few looking this good.

They entered the tent and Jessie appeared impressed. She had brought wine and told Brian in a breathy, sexy, low voice to put his wine away. Hers, she said, was special. Brian poured the wine and offered her a chair. He liked a little small talk to break the ice, although with Jessie, there seemed to be no ice to break. As he sipped wine, she began to remove her jacket. She did it in slow methodical movements that were already arousing Brian. Jessie stood up as she unbuttoned her lacy see-through blouse, her breasts looming large and inviting. Reaching behind her back she unhooked her bra and let it fall to the floor.

As Brian pointed to the array of fingernail polish, she shook her head and, in a deep sexy voice, said, "Now you." She licked her lips, moving her tongue slowly around her full, bright red mouth.

Brian gulped the rest of his wine and tore off his shirt. Sweat was beading on his forehead; his breath, quickening. Frantically undoing his belt, unzipping his pants and stepping out of them, he swaggered over and kissed her. Jessie returned the kiss with fervor, her tongue roaming salaciously in his mouth. He felt he had died and gone to heaven. That's the last thought he would have for quite some time.

As Brian's body hit the floor, Jessie grabbed his pants and removed his wallet. She already knew he liked to carry a large amount of cash. She had gleaned that from the many emails they had exchanged. There was also the cash he had brought to pay her after the sex he expected to have. After putting the cash and his credit cards in her purse, she was ready to leave. Sale of the credit card numbers would be completed before she got home. A phone call and money would be sent to her checking account.

Jessie laughed out loud, looking at Brian's crumpled body lying disheveled on the tent floor. "Men are so stupid, so brainless when it comes to women and sex," she quipped sarcastically.

Jesse was not naive when it came to men or sex. She had learned long ago how to control both—not that she always got the upper hand. Sometimes her encounters had placed her in horrible danger. She had learned from those escapades. A gun she carried in her bag had helped her out of a few precarious situations. She had never killed anyone, but she had wounded a sick excuse for a human once. He had managed to stay alive without going to a hospital, so no one had ever been the wiser. The guy had hopefully learned a valuable lesson.

She took one more glance at the still body, quickly checked the tent to make sure she had not left anything behind, hopped into her Cadillac, and headed for Duluth.

Brian awoke with a spitting headache and a fuzzy memory of what had happened. Recollections of the fabulous beauty who had joined him for sex and his subsequent awakening on the floor of his tent had his mind spinning. He hadn't realized what had happened until he saw his wallet on the floor. He knew then before even looking in it: He had been set up—a patsy for a robbery—a clandestine rendezvous that turned out to be a stinking set-up.

Brian pulled the sheets off the mattress and let the air out. He packed up the candles, potpourri, nail polish, and wine and took them to the car. Taking the tent down, he still couldn't believe what had happened. She could have killed him. Who would have been the wiser?

Cheryl had warned him about getting involved with people from the Internet. She was much more street savvy than he was. He should have listened. With his dreams of hot sex and his money and credit cards gone, Brian made his way home.

The anguish on his face prompted Cheryl to wrap her arms around him and welcome him home. As Brian gave her the blow-by-blow description of his night of anguish, she coaxed him to the couch and soothed his damaged ego with a soft kiss on his lips.

A call to the credit card company finally stopped the exploitation of his credit cards. They had already been used several times. The companies would have new ones in the mail the next day.

CHAPTER 14

"RING OF FIRE"

———◆———

RELISHING HER VICTORY OVER THE small area of kitchen counter, Roxanne's memory flashed to another place in her home that was not overwhelmed by stuff. It was full but the boxes were neatly stacked. She seemed to remember that there was a pathway around the room where the grayish blue carpet could still be seen. She hadn't ventured to the far end of the upstairs hallway in years. Actually, she hadn't even tried to navigate the steps to the upper floor in a long time.

The spare bedroom where her parents' belongings were stored hadn't been entered in years. When she and Charles first packed up the contents, Roxanne had been in that room almost every day. She had spent hours crying and touching her mother and father's possessions, feeling somewhat calmer, as though they were present when she sat among their things.

Eric's room was filled with memorabilia from his short life. Roxanne hadn't entered his room since his funeral and couldn't bring herself to go there even now—not yet.

Roxanne stood in dread as she thought of the long struggle to get up the stairway and then to the end of the long hallway where four large bedrooms lined the dark foreboding path.

Her slippers gave her no traction against the papers, books, and boxes that filled the steps to overflowing. She found the tennis shoes she wore outside and put them on, plotting a route up the menacing staircase.

Moving slowly down the long hallway was tiring and disturbing. Where did all the possessions come from? Did she actually bring all this rubbish into her house? And when did she accumulate such an abundance? It had seemed to appear overnight.

The door to the last bedroom on the right looked foreboding. Taking a deep breath and pushing the door slowly, she cringed as it squeaked and suddenly swung open. It took her breath away for a moment; she wanted to turn and run. She stood in the grip of fear, waiting for something else to happen, not knowing what.

The first thing she saw was the large, four-poster bed her parents had slept in for as long as she could remember. The heavy brown and beige bedspread and matching pillow shams were just as she had left them. The bed seemed waiting for someone to turn the covers down and crawl in.

Sorrow overcame her and she wept. Then, the sadness lifted, and she looked around the large room. Totes and boxes were piled high, but there was ample space to walk around. There was actually some order to this room, and Roxanne was surprised at the comfort it gave her. She carefully opened the closet door and touched the clothes her parents had valued. Her father's favorite black winter suit and several white shirts, still looking clean and recently pressed, hung in the closet next to his favorite black and white sweater. Her mother's brown fur coat and several pair of shoes and boots were there, too, looking as if she could just stop by, slip her feet into them, and walk away.

She lifted the lid of one tote and realized it must be her brother's. It had Brian's football in it and also one of his baseball gloves. High school memorabilia with yearbooks and graduation pamphlets were yellowed and smelled musty. As she pulled some things out, she noticed a small box held shut with a rubber band. When she took the band off, it opened. Inside were several bottles of nail polish. *What in the world was Brian doing with nail polish,* she wondered.

Roxanne walked over to the window and opened the curtain. It was still daylight, but the room was dark. The bright sun blinded her for a moment but then let her have a better look at her surroundings. Mice had found their way in. Although she didn't actually see any, she could see the damage they had done where they had chewed their way around the space. They weren't as plentiful as they were downstairs; and although she could see their destruction, she didn't have to see them running around up here.

Dust lay thick on every surface. The smell of old musty possessions filled the room. Roxanne slumped into a high back chair and plopped her feet onto the matching ottoman. She smiled and wished she had a cup of coffee or, better yet, a glass of wine to drink slowly while revisiting her nostalgia. Tears had dried on her face, and she was suddenly exhausted. It had been a journey for her—a long difficult trek up the stairs and down the long hallway. Emotions had run rampant, and she was weary.

Memories danced in her head—good memories of her youth and her parents, of her dear friends Billie and Charlotte, and the two men she had loved. Jack, of course, her first, would forever be her dearest love. Maybe he was so special because he was her first love, or maybe because her parents had forbidden their love. She had dreamed of running off with him, calling her mom and dad to say they had eloped.

Her second love, the man she had married, had been a charmer— a handsome well-educated man from a good family—'good' meaning rich. That was particularly important to her parents. He had probably truly loved her and had done his best to make her happy. "No, not probably," she said out loud with conviction. She knew he had certainly loved her.

There had been happy days, many actually. When the children were at home and when they had been involved with school and friends, their lives had been good. Also, Roxanne and Billie had enjoyed a lucrative therapy practice, so they were financially sound. *Why had she forgotten all the good times,* she wondered.

She was fully aware that her parents' deaths and later Eric's had sent her into an abyss from which she could not escape. Depression had engulfed her—hugged her tightly like a jealous lover and tightened its grip as each day passed. She soon had no fight left in her—no way to free herself from that beast.

She wondered why she hadn't sought help. She had helped many others. Years before, when the downward spiral had begun, she had tried to rein in collecting so much stuff. She had combed through her college textbooks, searching for an answer. It most certainly had been there, but she couldn't or wouldn't accept anything she read as relevant to her. Why she couldn't just ask for help remained a mystery. As memories of her illness replayed in her mind, she remembered Billie's pleas, begging Roxanne to let her help. *Perhaps therapists, like nurses and physicians, can't heal themselves,* she thought.

Their thriving practice continued without Roxanne for a while. Then Billie's husband died in a car accident and they were forced to close their practice. Billie had reassured Roxanne that their friendship had not ended though and tried many times to see her, but Roxanne had refused. By that time, paranoia had set in; and she was sure people were out to get her.

Past regrets and early accomplishments flooded Roxanne's mind. Sadness and happiness walked hand in hand through her thoughts. No—it had not been all bad: There had been many good days. Why had she forgotten those happy times? Why had she let the good be swallowed up by the bad?

She thought back on her conversation with Brian. Roxanne had held her ground; she had actually been the person in charge. Brian had retreated, and she had been the winner. It had felt wonderful, and now that same feeling came over her. She had stood up to him—had not folded under his threats and rants.

While Roxanne drifted into a weary sleep, a shadowy figure made its way through the wooded area that night, working ever closer to the house, moving quickly, and soon stood just outside the back entrance. Carrying two large cans, the firebug spread gasoline around the outside of the house. Using a long piece of wood thickly wrapped in rags he had soaked in fuel, the arsonist lit the torch and threw it on the dead grass next to the dwelling. Flames quickly engulfed the wooden structure.

The sound of barking dogs and the smell of smoke woke Roxanne. She was startled and for a moment couldn't move. It seemed as if she were caught up in a dream, not knowing if the noise and smells were real or merely a vision of sorts. It took a minute for her to remember where she was and what she had been doing. Pulling back the curtains, she could see someone moving around outside. Although the sky was cloudy, a sliver of moonlight occasionally peeked through, enough for her to glimpse an outline of someone. Suddenly she saw the roaring fire that had begun to engulf her home. She stood motionless in fear for just a second, and then her instincts kicked in. She had to get out…or die trying.

Opening the bedroom door she could see flames licking the wall and hear the crackling of combustibles at the end of the hall. Quickly shutting the door, she ran to the windows facing the flower garden. It was a long way down, and she was frightened. Reminding herself to stay calm, she thought of how to get out. Eric's room across the hall had been equipped with an escape ladder that, from practice with Eric when the house was built, would swiftly take her to the grass below. She had been agile then, and fearless.

"Will the ladder still be there?" Roxanne asked out loud, though she wouldn't know the answer until she was in Eric's room. She wrapped the old bedspread around herself and made a mad dash for the bedroom opening, then shut the door as fast as she could. She didn't have time for remorse or sad memories as she rushed to the window. The rope ladder was still there; at first the window wouldn't open, but, with a good shove, it gave way, and she threw the ladder out. It cascaded downward.

For just a moment she scanned the room. Memories came rushing back. Eric's quilt, so special, made from his high school football uniforms, and pictures on the wall: all whirled through her mind. His smiling face gave her courage, and he seemed to be right there with her.

Getting out the window and making her way down the swinging rope steps did not come easily, but Roxanne didn't even realize how difficult it was to navigate her escape. Her life was in danger, but her survival instincts were in full swing.

CHAPTER 15

"LEAN ON ME"

———

BILLIE HAD SEEN THE FIRE from the porch at Stonebridge. She hadn't been sure exactly where it was, but it appeared to be at her old friend Roxanne's house. She called the fire department, and the rescue squad and fire trucks were soon on the way with lights flashing and sirens blaring. She thought of Roxanne and her affliction. If the fire were at her home, it would devastate her. Billie knew all about hoarding. When she still had her practice, she had counseled several clients who had been plagued with that particular disorder. It would be overwhelming for Roxanne. Billie grabbed her keys and ran to her vehicle. Roxanne would need her, and she would need to be there for her longtime friend.

The piercing sounds of the emergency vehicles filled the summer evening on the lake. Roxanne was standing on the grass under Eric's window when the trucks arrived. She walked over to them—a stunned look on her face. A stiff breeze blew across the lake, and she was suddenly chilled. Bewildered, Roxanne clung to a fireman who promptly wrapped a blanket around her.

Within minutes Roxanne saw her dear friend Billie, half-walking half-stumbling over the lawn as she made her way toward her. They wrapped their arms around each other, filling the air with their sobs. They hadn't seen each other in so long; yet it felt like they had just been together the day before, laughing and talking.

"You'll come home with me," Billie said with quiet determination. Roxanne nodded, and, as soon as allowed, the two long-time friends began the walk to Billie's car. Billie opened the car door and Roxanne slid onto the seat. She sat in silence, stunned by the events of the last hour and overcome with emotion.

Once back at Stonebridge, Billie opened the car door and gently took Roxanne's hand. As she helped her out of the vehicle, she held her close and guided her into the porch overlooking the lake. "I'll get some wine," she said in a soft comforting voice. "You just sit here and relax. I'll be right back." Billie quickly poured the wine and found a couple snacks to go with it. She could see Roxanne trembling through the glass doors. Tears filled Roxanne's eyes, and she was soon sobbing. Billie put the glasses down and wrapped her arms around her friend. They wept together and sat quietly once their tears subsided. Silence felt comfortable between the two of them.

When the situation calmed, Billie brought her friend a nightgown and walked with her to a bedroom with twin beds. "I'll stay right here with you," Billie said as she turned the bed down for Roxanne. "You'll be safe and sound here with me. Nothing is going to hurt you."

Roxanne's eyes looked hollow and weary. She had barely escaped the fire in her home. Her dogs and cats had most likely burned to death, and her sanctuary—her place of safety—was gone.

Billie pushed her bed even closer to Roxanne's, and they lay holding hands until Roxanne's grasp let go. She had finally drifted off to sleep. Billie would keep a close eye on her until morning.

Fresh coffee and rolls filled the porch with a pleasant fragrance. Roxanne was up, wearing shorts and a tee shirt, courtesy of her dear friend.

Roxanne's mother's favorite quote had been, "Everything looks better in the morning," and it was so true. Last night's terror had ended; and sitting at the resort looking over the beautiful lake was a blessing. Roxanne sat silent for most of the morning. Billie occasionally asked how she was feeling and if she was sure she hadn't been injured while escaping her death trap. Those were the only interruptions. Later, after Billie had fed her a substantial lunch, the fire marshal stopped by.

Jack held Roxanne in a long hug when he first entered the sunny porch at the resort. They had a long history of friendship and love. He had always had a jittery feeling in his stomach when he thought of Roxanne. Their high school courtship had been abruptly ended by Roxanne's parents, but the fondness he had for her had continued.

"It was arson." Jack's statement was short and curt. With that statement Roxanne remembered the shadowy figure she had seen alongside her house.

"Arson," Roxanne gasped but nodded her head in agreement. "I did see someone walking along the house, but who would want to burn my house down? Who would want to harm me? I don't think I have an enemy in the world."

"An arson investigation squad will come from Duluth sometime this morning," Jack informed Roxanne. "They'll figure out what happened."

"Can I go back there?" she asked. "I need to look for my animals—see if any of them survived."

"It's still smoldering," Jack answered and again put his arms around her. "You can't get too close, but yes, I'll bring you there if you want."

Roxanne asked to borrow a jacket from Billie, and she and Jack were soon on their way to what was now a crime scene.

A brisk wind was fueling the persistent fire again. Smoke and debris from the smoldering house filled the air, and several volunteer firemen kept a watchful eye on the remains of the once beautiful house.

The stuff Roxanne had amassed in her living space was exposed for the entire world to see. There were spectators parked on the road, watching what was left of her life's possessions burn away. Several people in cars were looking through binoculars to get a closer look at the remains of the infamous hoarder house. An incredible sense of loss washed over her, and she sobbed into her hands. Jack pulled the car over before they had reached the house, wrapped his arms around her, and held her. He didn't say anything; he didn't need to.

She wanted to tell Jack to turn the car around and take her back to Billie's. The gawkers were watching them; and she felt like a freak on display, but she needed to look for her animals, so she had to be strong.

She held her head high as she stepped out of his car, searching the grounds for signs of her beloved animals. Roxanne didn't look at the other cars; she wouldn't give them the satisfaction of acknowledging they were even there.

One of the firefighters came toward them; and, as he approached, he reached into his coat and pulled out a little gray kitten. "It came meowing from the flowers behind the house. A dog is around here, too, but it was afraid to let me touch him."

Just then Duke came bounding from the back of the house, wagging his tail and snuggling up against Roxanne. Roxanne wailed out his name, tears of joy streaming down her face as she hugged her dear companion. Duke simply wagged his tail and licked her face. At least two of her animals had survived.

Walking around the ruins, Roxanne was struck with how detached she felt. This place had been home just 24 hours ago—her refuge from the world. Now she felt nothing—not even sadness—as she looked at a pile of rubbish that also meant nothing.

Jack helped her into the front seat as she cuddled the little kitten. He opened the back door for Duke who bounded into the seat. The smile on Roxanne's face made Jack feel fantastic. Satisfaction for each of them seemed to fill the car; a peaceful day was in store.

"Do you want to take a drive or go right back to the resort?" Jack's voice was cheerful; his mood, infectious.

"I'd love a drive. That would be a relief," Roxanne said, beaming as the words tumbled out quickly. Years ago they had driven down country roads in the magnificent forests surrounding Hidden Rapids. Itasca County was known for its many lakes and unforgettable beauty. Trails, campgrounds, picnic areas, and resorts enticed summer travelers to come and spend their money and time in the north country of Minnesota.

"We'll take a drive up Highway 38," Jack said enthusiastically. "You won't even recognize the road." He went on about the new highway. The old sharp twists and turns had been eased so cruising it now was easy. The scenery along the road had always been full of splendor. Frost hung heavily on the trees in early fall and again in the spring. As the weather cooled, fog rolled in to paint the leaves and branches. Spring brought budding foliage to life; green sprouts gave promises of warm days and cool nights. Before the leaves burst open, it was easier to see the lakes. Roads did not reach many of them. Four wheelers and foot traffic let the northern visitor witness the quiet serenity of a cold, clear lagoon nestled in what felt like the wilderness.

"We should have a picnic," Jack said smugly, impressed with his idea. "There's that store in Marcel. We'll buy some food there." He gave Roxanne a questioning look. She smiled and nodded her approval. The store in Marcel had all they needed. They bought hot dogs, buns, chips, and ice tea. They drove to Jack-the-Horse Lake. There a lovely stretch of sandy beach and picnic area welcomed them.

Jack started a fire to roast the hotdogs and talked of the odd name. They knew the story but it was fun to talk about it again. Jack-the-Horse McDonald got his name when he was a foreman for a large lumber camp. A weak, sickly horse had held up the logging team. So, McDonald stepped into the sick horse's place, enabling the team to haul its load back to camp. Henceforth he was "Jack-the Horse," never referred to otherwise in the woods. When McDonald assumed charge of operations on a nameless lake, his men simply tagged it in his honor. Everybody accepted the designation, and Jack-the-Horse Lake is on the map today.

They roasted their hotdogs and sat close together by the fire. Duke and Kitty played together. Roxanne was feeling so normal. She wasn't anxious or worried about anything. It was not like her usual days where even the thought of leaving her home or talking with someone other than Barry would have made her feel like throwing up. Her sense of normalcy bestowed a calm in her she had not felt in many years. Sadly, her pink cloud was short-lived; reality would set in soon.

CHAPTER 16

"THAT'S LIFE"

———◆———

BARRY KNEW HIS PROPOSED LAND deal had been set aside after the fire. Roxanne would naturally be too overwhelmed with insurance adjusters and police who were helping the arson squad investigate the fire to think of Barry's proposal. Her mental state was fragile, and Billie was determined to protect Roxanne as much as possible for as long as possible. She had been in touch with a mental health clinic in Duluth. They were aware of Roxanne's problem, and a therapist that Billie was well acquainted with was willing to travel to her.

Roxanne's situation was now totally different: she needed a house, a home to live in. The fire had forced her not only to vacate her house, it forced her to rejoin the outside world—to enter the human race again. It had also burned all of her *things*—her beloved *possessions*.

A highly regarded therapist, Sandra Walsh, would fly from Duluth to Hidden Rapids to meet with Roxanne. Roxanne was nervously pacing the floor in the living room when the therapist arrived. Billie accompanied Sandra into the great room of the lodge and introduced the two. The warmth of the fireplace helped Roxanne relax. Billie brought coffee and offered to stay with Roxanne. Her offer was appreciated, but Roxanne wanted to talk to Sandra alone. The mere fact that Billie trusted Sandra also gave Roxanne a sense of peace.

The two sat next to each other as Sandra asked questions. "These questions are to give you and me a sense of where you are in your illness," Sandra said, her voice kind and gentle. "I'm going to ask questions concerning your state of mind. There is no right or wrong answer. Please try really hard to reply honestly. How often do you feel miserable or sad?" Following the question Sandra offered her four possible answers: || *always* || *sometimes* || *often* || *never* ||

"Often," Roxanne replied, her manner unruffled.

Sandra went on to ask a series of questions, using the same set of replies. "Can you do the things you used to do? Do you get frightened or panicky for no apparent reason? Do you sleep well? Have you given up your friendships?"

The list of questions went on, and Roxanne diligently answered every one.

They touched briefly on her problem of hoarding. As Sandra wrapped up her session for the day, she called Dr. Armstrong to set up a complete physical for Roxanne the following week. She wanted Roxanne to have an overall exam, including chemical analysis, hormonal breakdown, and brain scan. "I want a total picture of you, not only your mental health—your thoughts, wants, fears, and regrets—but also your physical health."

"Hoarding has many components," Sandra said gently. "Together we will slowly peel away the many layers of your life. We'll take a look," she said with a smile, "a look—inside and out—to find the real Roxanne again."

Sandra said her goodbyes to the women. She would fly back to Duluth.

Billie had a quick snack ready for them: a nice, cold glass of lemonade and a bowl of chips. They did not talk about Roxanne's visit with the therapist.

Roxanne had rented one of the cabins at Stonebridge. Billie had not wanted anything for the use of the cabin, but Roxanne insisted on paying her own way.

Her cabin, named Sunny Skies, was rustic but comfortable. It had two bedrooms, a small bath with a shower, and an open area that was her living room, dining room, and kitchen. It had big windows overlooking the lake and a roomy deck with a grill, table and chairs, and two comfortable lounge chairs.

Her thoughts were mostly about the fire and the arsonist, thinking of who would perhaps want to kill her and her animals. But she also thought of Barry and the idea of selling and construction on part of her cherished property. Actually she did have to think about construction now. She needed a house.

Roxanne used the phone in her cabin to call Barry; his wife answered.

Suddenly feeling shy and intimidated, Roxanne took a deep breath to overcome her fear and said, "This is Roxanne. Is Barry there?"

"Yes…he's just getting up from the table. Hold on a minute."

Roxanne heard Barry's wife's hushed words, saying "It's Roxanne, Honey. I have to go. See you later."

"Hello, Roxanne," Barry boomed. "What can I do for you?"

"I need to see you—to talk to you. I'm sure you heard about the fire."

"I heard, Roxanne, and I'm so sorry. My calendar is at the lumberyard, but I'll call you to let you know when I have some free time—probably not until this afternoon. What's your number?"

Roxanne answered softly "I don't have a number—no cell phone yet. Billie is taking me to get one later this morning."

Their conversation ended, and Roxanne felt so far removed from the real world. Tears and a few minutes of self-pity passed. Shortly she was walking into the Stonebridge Lodge.

Billie greeted her with a smile and a wave as she finished checking in a customer. Within minutes the women were on the way to Hidden Rapids. Roxanne watched as Billie maneuvered her four-wheel-drive pickup. It had been so long since Roxanne had been behind the wheel of a vehicle, and the thought of ever driving again frightened her.

A landmark restaurant, The Harbor, was boarded up. Roxanne had read about the closure in the local paper, and Barry had told her about the owner's death and subsequent sales to others who could not make a profit running the restaurant. However, seeing this once beautiful restaurant, closed and needing repair, hurt her deeply. Summer on

Pokegama Lake had often meant stopping by The Harbor, first for gas for the boat and later for a cocktail and dinner. They would start their scrumptious meal with an order of deep fried cauliflower. Roxanne's favorite entrée had been the Harbor Special steak served with baked potato, house salad, and their popular Harbor House dressing. It had a hint of garlic, and Charles had always said that if she ordered that dressing, he would not kiss her good night.

She always ordered the dressing, and he always kissed her good night.

She smiled as she thought about all the good times. Sadly, however, her life turned sour when she had become focused on her things and the hurtful words her husband had said after her hoarding took control. But there had been good times. There had been laughter and hugs, kisses, and love, too.

Traffic in Hidden Rapids that day was bumper to bumper. It was summer, and tourists had arrived in full force. As they drove into town, Roxanne could not believe how things had changed. It was hard to grasp the transformation. New shops now lined the streets, replacing the old ones Roxanne had remembered. The outskirts of town were now home to three large box stores, a large theater, and numerous motels.

Stepping into the cell phone store, Roxanne felt like she was walking into the Outer Limits. However, that long ago TV show was fiction; this was reality. She did have a cordless phone at home; and she watched television, so she had seen cell phones; but to actually have one in her hand felt strange. The salesman was talking fast as he explained all the features of the latest smartphone. Billie spoke up quickly before he went on too long. She explained that this was Roxanne's first phone and that he would need to slow down and explain the workings of the mysterious unit carefully.

Roxanne left the store feeling bewildered and overwhelmed, but Billie had assured her that she would help, that before long she would be not just using the cell phone but would actually love it.

Roxanne suddenly felt frightened. She had managed to talk to the clerk, but that was with much coaxing from Billie. Feeling particularly unnerved, she wanted to go home—home to her lake—to her old life. It had been her home forever, and she would never be happy away from it. Even though she hadn't taken advantage of the wonderful things the water offered for a long, long time, she could never be away from it.

CHAPTER 17

"I'LL GET BY WITH A LITTLE HELP FROM MY FRIENDS"

———◆———

ALTHOUGH ROXANNE HADN'T LEARNED TO use her new cell phone's many functions, she did know how to make a call. As she tapped the numbers on the phone that put her in touch with the lumberyard, her stomach felt uneasy; she hoped she would not be ill.

"Anderson Lumber…"

"Hello, Barry?" Roxanne asked, wondering if she had gotten through to the right person.

"This is Barry. Is that you, Roxanne?"

"Yes, it is. I just got a phone and I'm not comfortable with it yet. I'm wondering if I ever will be," she said, laughing at herself. The phone felt like a foreign object in her hand. Nothing about it looked like the phone she had used for years. She felt afraid even to touch it. "I'd like to see you. I'm back at the resort, and we have unfinished business to talk about."

Barry's heart jumped as she talked. "Unfinished business," she had said. Could the proposal he had brought to her still be alive? He had all but written it off after the fire. Considering her fragile state and all the trauma of the fire, Barry had no hope of buying her property.

"How would you like to have lunch at Central School? It's been converted from a school to an emporium with an eatery, an art gallery, and some craft shops. The café serves tasty soups and sandwiches, and the atmosphere is really appealing." Barry's upbeat attitude actually made her feel a bit excited.

"I'd love to, but I have to ask you to pick me up. My car burned in the fire, and actually I haven't driven in years." Roxanne could hear the excitement in his voice as he agreed to pick her up at Stonebridge and they talked of a time.

"That was Roxanne!" Barry yelled to his dad who had just walked in the door. "She's going to have lunch with me today at Central School. I thought my proposal was totally off the table, but I think she might be considering it."

"Just be careful with her," Jack told his son. "Any kind of pressure could send her into an abyss."

"I'm going to be really gentle with her," Barry assured his father. "I know you have a soft spot for her, and she has become a very good friend to me also. I never told you, but when I was first married and money got a little tight, she always seemed to slip a little extra in my pay envelope for yard work. It was as if she knew I was short of cash. I would never hurt her."

Jack gave his son a pat on the back and wished him good luck.

Barry hadn't been to the resort for quite some time, but it had always impressed him. He knew there had been condos built recently because their lumberyard had provided the materials. There was a time when he had driven the delivery truck and had delivered many loads to Stonebridge.

When he had worked and learned enough, his dad let him begin learning how to become a building estimator. He loved learning formulas and working with the contractors. He had actually learned more about the building business than he thought. His dad would often ask him questions to test his knowledge, and Barry had been surprised by what he knew. He had learned without realizing it through on-the-job training.

Contractors often thought they were the only ones who needed an estimate—or a delivery for that matter. Builders wanted their materials

ASAP. They'd think a note saying Rush on the order actually meant something. Barry didn't want to be the one to tell them it meant absolutely nothing. They expected to be courted and cajoled, flattered to retain their business. They also wanted to be taken to lunch occasionally, and they wanted salesman to visit job sites on a regular basis. Although a phone call to the lumberyard would get a delivery rolling, they would prefer that sellers would come to them, make a list of their needs, and even oversee their deliveries if possible.

Barry pulled into a parking spot in front of the lodge. The screen door was closed, but he could see Billie and Roxanne sitting at the table. He softly knocked on the door and heard a friendly "Come in" from Billie.

Roxanne looked so different from their last visit. Her hair was clean and styled; and she was dressed in a perky spring outfit. She actually gave Barry a hug, and he reciprocated. He helped her into the car and they were off. She had visited with him over the years and seemed to be at ease. Actually, he had been the only one she had spoken to in a very long time. Roxanne even mentioned the fire and losing all her things. She brought up the yard and the beautiful flowers that had been trampled by the firefighters. She wasn't upset about the destruction of the flowers but rather just telling him what had happened to all his hard work.

The look on her face was priceless as she got out of the car and walked the beautiful curved staircase to the third floor of the old school house. The café was cozy, and the smell of vegetable soup filled the air. Barry poured coffee into the cups they picked up by the counter—classic roast for her and French Roast for him—and selected a table. The young waitress rattled off countless choices of sandwiches, obviously overwhelming Roxanne. So Barry ordered for her, and Roxanne quietly thanked him.

Large windows overlooked downtown Hidden Rapids, and Roxanne was taking it all in. Years had passed since the last time she had been in the city center. She had talked to herself before Barry picked her up.

She had felt fearful and had to stop the tears that had welled up in her eyes. Billie had assured her that she didn't have to go—that Barry would understand if she needed more time to venture out in the real world.

The old Roxanne had appeared, for just a second or two, but she promised herself she could handle this. More encouragement from her dear and trusted friend Billie had given her strength. She called on that now as she and Barry sat by a large window overlooking the streets below. A few customers greeted Barry as they walked in. No one seemed to know who she was, nor care for that matter. Roxanne was glad they took no notice; her self-conscious feelings subsided. As they sipped their coffee and ate lunch, she was mentally choosing the right words to tell Barry.

"I've decided: I *will* sell you a lakeshore lot to build your spec house." The words came plain and simple.

Barry's jaw dropped. Roxanne went on to say she needed a new home also; and, with a huge grin, she said her home had to be the first one built.

Barry's excitement could not be hidden, and he didn't even try. He grabbed her hand, kissed it, and thanked her. As they finished lunch, he suggested they stop by the lumberyard to pick up house plan books for her to look at. He would normally have suggested their website but knew Roxanne had never used a computer.

Jack was pleasantly surprised to see Barry and Roxanne walk in. He was on his feet, welcoming them with a hello and a hug for Roxanne. She responded with a hug back and suddenly felt a part of the world. Thoughts of her special problems flashed in her mind, and she knew there were enormous struggles she would have to battle. However, for this moment—this minute—she felt strong and peaceful; and she basked in it.

Barry pulled books from the shelf in his father's office and brought them to Roxanne. She loved the feel of them, but another flash of her home came into her mind: books, magazines, and newspapers stacked in piles falling around her stopped her hand in mid air from reaching for them. The vision frightened her and she shook her head.

"I'll just take one," she said in a whisper. "I will need an arrangement that has three bedrooms and three baths...and I know I'll want a large deck to enjoy the lake view."

"Okay," Barry said quickly. As he searched through the shelves for the right book, he came up with two, glanced through them, and handed her a thick book with a picture of an elegant house on the cover.

Barry got a call from a contractor just as he was ready to return Roxanne to the resort. "I'll take her back," Jack told Barry enthusiastically. The smile on Roxanne's face let Jack know she approved.

Jack helped Roxanne into his pick-up. It was a one-ton that was hard to get into. Even with the grab bars, he had to boost her up to the seat. They laughed as he awkwardly tried to help her. They chatted on the way to Stonebridge, and Roxanne had a real sense of herself—at least who she used to be. It may have been fleeting, but it was definitely an ah-ha moment.

I could be normal. She let the thought cascade over her. *The fire has given me another chance at life; it has forced me to take chances.* She wanted to cry, to share her excitement with Jack, but she contained herself. Her road to recovery would be frightening, time consuming, and, if she were honest with herself, riddled with doubts. It had taken her a long time to fall into the dungeon of hoarding. She knew the state of mind that had produced the illness would not be easily cured—but maybe it could be managed.

Intellectually, Roxanne knew what had to happen. She had to tackle the trauma of her loss, but handling her feelings was a different story. She would have to delve into herself, her emotions over losing her parents and Eric. The thought of even remembering that pain already hurt her to the core.

Jack stopped the pick-up in front of the lodge, walked around to Roxanne, and opened the door. She half slid into his arms, and he steadied her as her feet touched the ground. He called out a hello to Billie, reached for Roxanne's hand, and squeezed it.

"Stay and have a glass of wine with us." Billie's invitation was welcomed. Jack and Roxanne settled onto a comfortable sofa in the lodge's living room. Rustic beauty surrounded them. The two-sided fireplace lent its beauty to both the dining room and living room. The day had cooled, and the warmth of the fireplace felt especially comfortable.

Billie and Stone soon joined them. As the conversation turned to Roxanne's decision to build, she expressed concern as to where she would live while construction took place. Billie had offered her a home, but Roxanne wanted a place of her own. She didn't want to overstay her welcome, and the cabin she was renting now had been rented to several others during the summer.

Jack had a solution. He offered the apartment above his boathouse for her temporary residence. Roxanne could keep a close eye on the project and also be close enough to help Billie some at the resort. He went on to say that Roxanne needed something to keep her busy. Roxanne agreed about her wanting to help Billie but laughed, saying how the gossips would really be in full swing if they lived that close to one another.

Jack said good-bye and urged her to give his offer consideration. He thanked Billie for her hospitality and told Roxanne he would call her in the morning.

Roxanne and Billie continued relaxing by the fireplace, enjoying another glass of wine. Roxanne had wondered how to begin this conversation but just decided to ask outright. "I hear you are ill." Roxanne voice was hushed with concern.

Billie laughed, and then replied, "You are a hermit—reclusive—and you have already heard about my health problems." They each laughed now and touched their glasses in a toast of solidarity.

"Barry told me," Roxanne explained. "He was my lifeline—my resource to the outside world. I just want you to know I care about you and will be there for you."

The two old and dear friends now sat silently enjoying the ambiance of the fire and renewal of a cherished friendship.

"I couldn't live above Jack's boat house," Roxanne stated, breaking the silence, and, with a laugh, went on to explain that it would give people too much to talk about. Although most would no longer remember they were once an item, she remembered, and it would feel odd.

Barry locked the lumberyard, walked to his car, and slid onto the seat. He drove to his home with the music loud and grinning from ear to ear. He hugged his wife hard as soon as he entered his home. "What's up?" she asked, hugging him back. "Your meeting must have gone well."

"Well!" he said, "It was fantastic...it was superbly wonderful!"

Barry didn't use that kind of expression ever. He danced his wife around the room and said, "We're going out to dinner. Is it okay if I ask Dad to come along?"

Barry's wife was glad to include Jack and loved to see Barry this excited. Jack was thrilled, too, and wanted to talk about Roxanne and her new home.

Before long the revelers were sitting at the Beachcomber. It was Saturday night, and the crowd was large. Prime rib was one of the specialties served only Friday and Saturday nights. That's what they would have, served with delicious popovers for which the restaurant was known. It was a true celebration marked with a champagne toast. Barry and Jack each ended the evening with Roxanne on their minds.

CHAPTER 18

"I FEEL PRETTY"

———————

EMILY WAS ON THE PHONE most of the day making appointments. She would need a massage, manicure, pedicure, facial, eyebrow wax, and hairstyle. Emily wanted *the works* on Friday—the day the festivities for the class reunion began. Thursday she was off to Duluth for the afternoon. It was a one-and-a-half-hour drive and had a mall at the top of the hill where she could certainly find the perfect clothes. Friday night would be semi-casual. One didn't have to dress up, but the real casual night would be Saturday when a pig roast would feed the crowd. Friday, starting with 1948, three years of classes would join together at one of the many restaurants in the area. Emily's 1995, and also the '94 and '93 classes, would meet at The Drumbeater, a restaurant nestled on the shoreline of Pokegama Lake.

Driving to Duluth was another nostalgic journey. It had been a long time since Emily had driven on Highway 2 rolling through La Prairie, Blackberry, Warba, Swan River, and Floodwood. The feeling of being home in the North Country swept through Emily's mind.

The shops in Duluth did not disappoint her. Emily found a turquoise shirt that said "Life is better on the beach" in bold white letters on the front. A pair of white skinny jeans, white flip-flops glamorized with an array of colored sparkles, and long flashy turquoise earrings finished the ensemble. She loved it.

Emily drove back to Hidden Rapids, feeling smug about the clothes she had found and the way she looked in them. Her confidence surging, she decided to join vacationers by a huge fire at the beach. As she walked toward the fire, she was surprised and excited to see an old friend from high school. Shane had been Jenny's and her diehard swim meet supporter. He was considered a geek at school—a nerd—bright but withdrawn. He had often been teased and harassed by one particular bully named Scott Turner. Scott loved to intimidate anyone he could; it made him feel superior. He had loved to persecute the new seventh graders by blocking their way in the halls, making them late for class. If a new student asked for directions, he intentionally told them the wrong way to go.

Emily became *romantically* involved with Scott one night. Drinking had numbed her senses and clouded her judgment. He was as handsome as the day was long, and there had never been a shortage of girls in his life. Emily had been caught up in her *acting out* days and ended up as one of his conquests. With therapy she had stopped blaming him and had taken responsibility for her own actions; but she still felt revolted at the thought of him. He had used her for sexual gratification, and she had used him for attention. Emily had accepted the situation and moved on—or at least thought she had.

As she approached the beach partiers, Shane saw her and immediately walked toward her. The hug he gave her almost squeezed the breath out of her, and she laughed while trying to say hi. Her words came out in a whisper. He picked her up and swung her around flamboyantly, taking her completely by surprise. Stone walked over as their chaotic reunion took place.

"You've changed!" Emily said when she finally had breath again to speak.

"Well," Shane said, as he placed Emily's feet on the ground but continued to hang on to her. "I needed to change. That shy boy had to leave and grow up." He laughed now and let go of Emily.

"What would you like to drink?" he said, changing the subject.

"I'll have a margarita," Emily answered, shaking her head in disbelief and smiling.

Stone walked over and sat down by Emily. Shane returned shortly with a margarita on the rocks. The ambience created by the sunset on the glistening blue waters of Pokegama was priceless. Shane talked about the all-school reunion and how friends had encouraged him to attend. He was a forensic scientist and medical examiner for the Minnesota Bureau of Criminal Apprehension. As their conversation continued, Emily learned that he had never married but lived in Eden Prairie, Minnesota, and also enjoyed running in marathons.

Emily had not realized how handsome he was, although his looks had not changed much since high school. She had thought of him as a friend—a bit of a nerd, but always a nice guy.

The evening soon ended. Shane had rented a room at the lodge for the next four nights, and, as he said goodnight, he said he planned to see her tomorrow. He asked if she had heard that many were getting together at the Beachcomber Friday late afternoon before the reunions actually started. She had heard but wasn't keen on attending. However, with Shane and Stone's encouragement, she had agreed to be there.

Emily returned to her cabin with a jumble of thoughts running through her mind. Coming home was getting more interesting and enjoyable. Her shower was noisy, and putting up with the squeaky ceiling fan unnerved her. But sleep finally came.

A knock on the door woke her. Pulling back the curtain, she saw Shane standing there with Billie's famous cinnamon rolls and coffee. She talked to him through the window, telling him she would open the door as soon as she grabbed a robe. Emily hid her irritation; but for one thing, she was not eager to be up this early; and for another, she did not want to be seen by Shane with no makeup and her hair looking like she had put it in a blender. Emily was fussy. She had tried to change, but she had not succeeded. She was finicky.

The coffee party Shane had planned didn't go exactly like he wanted. Emily drank her coffee and ate the delicious roll, but she had appointments. She didn't have time to chit chat or hang out.

The spa treatment she had ordered began with a massage. The wonderful movements of the strong masseuse, rubbing and manipulating Emily's sore muscles, made her groan with bliss. Later, a facial soothed the headache she had experienced since the night before. Perhaps it was Shane or maybe the margarita. Whatever the cause, the masseuse worked it away.

Next was the facial. Soothing warm moisturizer led her thoughts to a tranquil place. Her jaw relaxed and tender fingers rubbing across her forehead, temples, and around her eyes put her into a totally serene state of mind. A helping hand moved her feet and helped her to an almost sitting position before assisting her to a soft leather chair. The water for the pedicure was warm and sudsy, and Emily, still feeling drowsy, relaxed and tried to stay awake. When asked about a color for her toes, Emily mumbled, "Choose it for me."

When it was time for her manicure, Emily had come back to reality. What a day she had experienced. Morning coffee and rolls with Shane... she loved the way it now made her feel just thinking about him. He was fascinating. She had known him in his younger days, but this certainly wasn't the guy she and Jenny had spent so many hours with as he watched and cheered them on. He was different, but then so was she. She was not the bubbly teenager or the rebellious young woman she had been. She was older and hopefully wiser.

The next part of her beauty treatment day would be a wash and style. The stylist was young. Her brown hair was short and spiked with a blue streak across the front. She had pierced eyebrows and lips. As she spoke, Emily could see the gold stud on her tongue. A red rose tattoo with a long green stem extended onto her fingertips.

"I want a trendy look," Emily stated with a smirk on her face. "Can you make me look twenty again?" she asked with a twinkle in her eye.

"I'm not a magician," the young woman said laughing, "but I can make you look great. Is that enough?"

"That will be perfect." The hairdo was a good style for her. The stylist had trimmed her hair a little, leaving enough for a short ponytail or a clip so she could get it off her face. Some highlights and low lights had been added, and a lighter color around Emily's face softened her features.

The pro began her final course of make-up with the explanation of what she was using. The makeup had a demi-matte finish with air-light texture—not heavy and not shiny. Emily was assured it would last all evening. Emily's lipstick would be a bold classic red paired with a smoky eye shadow. Waxing her eyes brows never felt good, but it did clean up the rogue hairs that seemed more prevalent with every birthday. A spray on makeup extender would keep the look fresh all night.

Emily felt like a new woman as she left the salon. During the drive home she turned on the music that had been popular in her last years of high school. She was getting in the mood for reacquainting with her co-horts—her partners in crime. She cheerfully waved to Stone and Shane as she drove into the lodge parking area, rolled the window down, and asked how soon they would be going to the Beachcomber.

CHAPTER 19

"YESTERDAY WHEN I WAS YOUNG"

OKAY, SHE WAS READY. SHANE had wanted her to ride with him, but Emily preferred having her own transportation. She wanted the freedom to come and go as she wanted without having to rely on anyone else. She trusted herself not to drink too much and not go places that she hadn't expected.

Stone was bringing Kirsten, and he had also offered her a ride. The parking lot at the Beachcomber was filling up fast. Emily pulled her small car into a space between two large trucks. She felt a little nervous as she left her car and started for the entrance. However, when Shane gently touched her shoulder and, with a smile, opened the door for her, her whole face conveyed how glad she was to see him.

Emily's eyes searched for familiar faces in the dim light. Shane asked what she would like to drink, and he headed for the bar. As Emily looked for a place to sit, Kirsten waved at her. She and Stone had arrived just minutes before them and had saved a table in the center of the barroom. Smiles, waves, and hugs were plentiful as people—some older, some younger—from several different graduation classes had gathered.

Time flew as stories of youth sprinkled with laughter and even a few tears enveloped the groups of people. There was standing room only. Emily excused herself and headed to the restroom, where she came face to face with Scott Turner. He grinned and whispered in her ear, "Pour me another Tequila, Sheila, and lay back and love me again."

She wanted to slap him but tried to ignore the snake and to move along toward the restroom. He grabbed her arm and said it again, a little louder this time. However, Shane was suddenly standing in front of Emily. He had pushed himself between the two and stood nose to nose with Scott. Scott turned and quickly walked away.

"Thanks. He's a mistake from the past," Emily remarked casually to Shane and then finished her trek to the powder room.

The bar was clearing out when she got back to her friends. They were soon going to The Drumbeater to meet with their classmates and three other classes. The reunion menu was simple: burgers and hotdogs with all the trimmings. The class presidents introduced the visiting teachers and those students who had won regional or state titles in their sports as well as academic achievements, were recognized. Emily was given a huge round of applause and a hug from her former swimming coach, noting the many trophies she and Jenny had brought home for the school. She missed Jenny more than ever that very minute.

Hugs, smiles, and even a few tears were the order of the evening. Memories of enthusiasm, naiveté, and the confidence of their youth seemed to wrap a circle around the graduates as they remembered the good, the bad, and–yes–sometimes the ugliness of being immature. Recollections of hurtful comments and thoughts of being left out were openly discussed. Those whose comments had been hurtful appeared to have been oblivious to the repercussions of their remarks, and those who made them were now truly sorry for their behavior.

Scott Turner even made his way over to Emily and Shane to offer an excuse for his rude behavior earlier in the evening. He blamed booze for his vulgar words. Shane heard his explanation and quickly replied "Alcohol doesn't change you, it reveals you." That said, Shane and Emily walked away.

It was time to say good night. Shane had stayed close to Emily throughout the evening but not too near. He had kept a watchful eye on her, observing her and those around her while also enjoying his own classmates.

Shane walked her to her car, which was still tucked in between two big trucks. "I wish you would have let me drive you," he said as he opened the car door. "I'm going to follow you back to the resort."

"Okay thanks. I'd appreciate that."

The trip to Stonebridge went fast. Shane watched her park her car, open her cabin door, walk in, and wave goodnight.

Emily readied for bed and let the memory of this fabulous night wash over her. She had been so worried about meeting her old classmates. No one, except for Scott Turner, had even alluded to her sometimes misbehaving during her senior year. She had felt welcomed, and that left her in a giddy mood.

She slowly removed her makeup, being careful to study exactly how it had been done. She wanted to be able to do it just like the stylist had for the next night. Her hair would not get mussed; she could sleep almost sitting up when she wanted her 'do' to last.

Her friends had decided to meet for lunch at Zorbaz. The restaurant sat on the banks of Pokegama Lake. The weather was forecast to be warm and sunny, so they would sit outside on the deck. Emily would dress casually for her lunch and the pig roast that evening. It would take place at the fairgrounds and would include all the classes.

She walked to the lodge in the morning. Billie had wanted to hear all about her reunion. Billie had had her class reunion at the Sugar Lake Lodge. Roxanne had declined the invitation, still struggling with her emotions; a large gathering was not something she felt she could handle yet. Jack had decided to skip the reunion, too, and instead spent the evening with Roxanne.

The smile on Roxanne's face that morning told the story. She and Jack had enjoyed a quiet time together. Jack had cooked steaks on the grill, and Roxanne had baked potatoes and made a delicious salad. They had also reminisced and savored memories of their youth.

After coffee and rolls, Emily walked back to her cabin to get ready for lunch with the girls. She had great looking legs and would show them off by wearing white short shorts and a coral tube top. The drive across the Pokegama causeway sparked more memories; she slowed the car, opened the windows, and breathed in the wonderful smell of the water. Zorbaz sat just on the other side of the bridge; and as she turned in, she saw her friend Sarah parking her car. They walked in together, arms around each other. Sarah had been on the swim team also; and although she was not as strong a swimmer as Jenny and Emily had been, she was quick and had been the lead on their relay swim team.

The six young women laughed and joked over lunch. The silliness and giggling that had been such a part of their youth took over once more, as though time had stood still. Over Bloody Marys and pizza, they talked of old boyfriends, teachers, and high school dances. They all felt fantastic.

Emily had all their phone numbers and they had decided to text and meet somewhere in the fairgrounds. The Saturday night reunion was scheduled to start at 5:00. There would be bars set up and happy hour until 6:00 when the meal would be served. Hogs were already turning on spits—the aroma from the drippings on charcoal evident several blocks away.

Shane and Stone were sitting outside when Emily drove up. Shane walked over and asked her to join them for a glass of lemonade. Kirsten was getting off early; they would soon head for the fairgrounds.

"I'll just stay for a few minutes. I have to look good for tonight."

"You already look good," Shane said.

Emily coyly smiled back. Actually, she knew she looked good, but she would look even better when she arrived that night. After a little small talk, she made her way to the cabin. Her hair looked pretty good and would take just a little tweaking. Makeup would take longer, and she still had to iron her jeans.

Emily again wanted to drive herself. Shane tried to convince her that he would leave whenever she wanted and stay as long as she wanted, but she was still adamant about wanting to have her own vehicle.

The parking lot at the fairgrounds was already packed, so she had to walk a long way to the festivities.

Music from the 1940s to 2015 filled the fairgrounds and spread to the houses far from the party. Emily danced with several old friends and also Ralph Jordahl, her junior year English teacher. As she respectfully called him Mr. Jordahl, he told her he was only a few years older than she. As teenagers, Emily and her friends had thought of their teachers as old people when actually they were probably about 24.

Laughter, talking, and dancing took center stage and the evening quickly flew by. Hugs and promises to keep in touch were bringing an end to the magnificent reunion. The turnout had been beyond expectation, and the planners were pleased that their hard work had been so well received.

Shane had grown weary of the dancing and drinking and had left the commotion and chaos of the hangers-on. He had tried to talk her into coming with him; he would drop her off at her car. However, she declined, saying she wanted to stay a little longer. She did not want the evening to end. Stone and Kirsten were still there; they said they would leave when Emily did.

About half an hour later, Stone saw Emily close to the entrance and told her that Kirsten was using the restroom and then they were leaving.

"Okay, but I'm going to my car now," Emily said. Stone encouraged her to wait until they could all walk together, but Emily felt fatigued and just wanted to leave.

"Hurt Her Once For Me"

EMILY FELT A STRONG ARM around her throat. The Half Nelson choked her, and she struggled to breathe. Her world and senses melted into oblivion as she hit the floor.

"Wait a minute. You brought the wrong one—the wrong girl!" Emily heard the soft voice say in an agonizing tone.

"What do you mean?" the other thundered.

"This isn't the woman who was with Stone. How could you make such a mistake?"

"Well, this is the one who was talking to him when we walked outside. They said something like 'have a good evening' or 'good to see you' and I just assumed…."

"You know what assume means: It makes an ass out of you and me."

The two tried to come to terms with their mistake. "Okay, she's the wrong one—so what? We'll get the right one next time. In the meantime we'll enjoy this special gal; she's awfully pretty.

When Emily awakened, she was strapped to a gurney, with tape over her eyes and mouth. The smell of fingernail polish filled her nostrils. Someone was gently removing her polish. The hand that held her fingers was soft—too large for most women but so supple. Emily moaned as the ache in her head came to life. She tried to scream but could only make a soft muffled sound. Someone with a whispery voice patted her hand and told her to be calm, assuring her she wasn't going to be hurt.

Emily moaned again and tried to talk, wanting to ask why someone was doing this. She was not trained in law enforcement, but she had watched her share of police shows. "I Survived" was one of her favorites. She had never considered, however, that she could someday be one of the victims. She concentrated on calming herself and started to let her senses do their job. There was an echo even though her kidnapper spoke in a whisper. That told her the building she was in was large and almost empty. The song, "Sweet Nothings," by Brenda Lee could be heard softly in the background. Emily also heard the captor talking either to himself or to an accomplice.

"I just want to make your hands pretty," the whispered voice said. "I've been thinking about this for a long time." The *nail technician* moved on to the next hand. When he was finished, he began to remove her toenail polish. "Do you want to do the pedicure?" he asked in a hushed and unfeeling voice. "I've already picked out polish I want to use for the manicure. It's called *My Chihuahua Bites.*

Emily felt a sudden pain on her arm between her shoulder and elbow. He had bitten her.

"Don't hurt her—not yet," a thunderous voice suddenly boomed and echoed through the building.

"I just wanted to hurt her once—just one time I want to be the one to cause the first pain. I want to hear her cry," the *technician* murmured.

"Well, *I'm* going to paint her toes," a louder voice replied. "I'm going to use *Pink Before You Leap*, and *I* will be the one to hurt her—just like always. You're not going to change the rules now, are you—after all this time? We have a routine! Let's not change now."

"It just doesn't match the color I am using for her fingers, but I guess it really doesn't matter. I can live with it." With a quiet giggle, he added, "*I'll* live with it, but she won't."

Emily felt her shoe being slipped off, and then warm water on her bare feet, followed by drying with a soft towel. Soon a gentle hand began smoothing lotion on and between her toes. *What the ----? I'm getting a bona fide pedicure,* she thought. Her foot was being soaked and massaged. There was another strong smell. The guy was removing the color on her toenails.

"I think she's wearing *Schnapps Out of It,* and I do like that color, but I was in the mood for a lighter, softer shade," he said matter-of-factly and unemotionally.

Emily wondered about the bizarre conversation she had just heard, but then it was all strange. She couldn't cry out. The tape across her mouth was thick and tight. She couldn't move her arms, but she continued to think—to plan a way out.

The tape around her eyes was so tight it felt as if her eyes were being forced into her skull. It was wrapped all the way around her head and pulled her hair as she tried to move. She knew if they took the blindfold off—if she saw them—she was certainly dead. Maybe they would kill her anyway.

Then more terror flowed through her as she felt her jeans being pulled down, then off. Her underwear was yanked off, and she felt cold air from her waist down. Terror surged through her body, and she thought she was going to throw-up as she was totally exposed from the waist down. Just as quickly as she was uncovered, she felt panties being slipped back on her—then something around her waist—a long, soft, drapy skirt maybe.

"I chose a pair of blue thong panties and a dark blue skirt," the person with the soft airy voice said.

"I have a light blue camisole and white and blue lace sweater," the man with the loud rough voice replied.

With that exchange they complimented each other on the trendy and beautiful ensemble they had created. They reminisced about the fashionable outfit they had seen on the mannequin in the store window and had decided then and there that it would be their next prey's outfit. Their laughter followed their congratulations on another abduction well done and with little fanfare. Their amusement continued until both were laughing hysterically. They talked of the name they should have for their surreptitious company—deciding, as their amusement continued, it should be named Snatch-Sex-Slay.

"We could put it on a card and pass it around—maybe we'd have others who'd like to partake in the fun."

"Nope," said the rough voice. "It should be Snatch-Slay-Sex. I don't want them until they *are* dead, and if you're in a certain mood, you don't want them at all. All you want to do is their nails, put a dress or skirt on them, and take pictures with them."

The room again filled with laughter, then became quiet, the tone of the voices more businesslike.

"She looks likes a princess—almost ready for pictures," the hushed voice spoke again.

"I wish you didn't have to be *in* the pictures," the forceful voice rang out. "It's something that could trace this to you...then to me."

"No one is ever going to see the pictures," the soft voice assured. "They're stashed safely away—hidden in a place where no one would ever look."

"Well, I sure hope so. If not—if anyone ever finds them, we are dead meat and off to prison we go."

"I try not to think about what it would be like to be locked up in a cell surrounded by criminals."

"So what do you think *we* are? We kill women—lots of them—without a moment's regret."

"I have regrets sometimes." The soft-spoken person's voice quivered, seeming to stifle a sob.

"Well, I don't," the other said gruffly. "The women wanted rough sex. They asked for it in their emails, so they got it."

"This young girl didn't ask for it," the first one said. "She didn't want any of what we offered. She didn't even find us on the Internet."

"No, but she wanted Stone, and you want him in prison, so let's get on with it. We're going to enjoy it—we both know that."

Emily could not stop the fear that raced in her brain. She thought she actually might die from fright, but that would also be a way out—to die before the murder occurred. And maybe that would be a blessing.

"It looks like you're ready, so let me take pictures of the two of you. Get her down and I'll get the camera."

Emily felt her legs being lifted up and turned. They were hanging off the edge of whatever she was lying on. She felt hands under her arms, setting her up and pulling her down onto the floor. They had put stilettos on her feet and she could barely stand, her ankles wanting to give way and twist. Her horror continued with an arm around her, the noise of a camera clicking, then a bright flash.

Shortly Emily heard a printer running. "I love the pictures. You were right, buddy. Even if she is the wrong one, we'll still enjoy her," remarked the soft-spoken man.

"I can't hang around much longer. Are you staying with her?"

"No, I should go, too, if you're not going to kill her right now. I'll strap her on the table again, and you can take your pleasure later."

"Okay, I'll help you; I don't want her getting loose."

Emily was lifted once again onto the hard surface of some kind of table or hard surface. Heavy straps again surrounded her arms and her legs. She could hear the ratchet tightening the straps and feel the material cutting into her arms. The long skirt she wore at least helped cushion the taut band that held her legs.

The building she was in was cold. The camisole and lacy sweater did not provide any warmth. *Maybe I'll just freeze to death; that would be an easy way out,* she thought. She had read about being out in the cold—of taking off clothes because the feeling of being warm overcomes you. *I could go that way,* she continued thinking. Her mind had been so full of what she had heard and the craziness of the kidnappers that she hadn't had time to think. Now she did and prayers filled her head. She was reminded of a plaque that she had hanging in their cabin. She had taken it down because the nail it hung on was about to pull out of the wall; but she intended to hang it up again once she found a different spot to pound the nail. It had said, "The will of God will never take you where the grace of God will not protect you." She prayed for that protection now.

Sleep came to her exhausted mind and body; but some sound woke her, and in a second, the memory of where she was and what had been happening came roaring back. A barely audible voice said what sounded like, "Oh...My...God!" Someone unlashed her hands and feet from the table, set her upright, and carried her away. She was flopped into the back seat of a vehicle and driven away from her place of terror. She wondered if this was the end of her nightmare or the beginning of a different one. If she was being rescued, why were her hands still bound and her mouth and eyes still covered with duct tape?

Emily found her wits and could feel the car seat with her cheek. It felt and smelled like leather. She also tried to pay attention to where the car was taking her. The road was gravel, then tar. The door opened and Emily was pulled out and helped to stand, the binding on her hands loosened. She heard the car door open and close, then the sound of the car driving away.

Emily carefully pulled the tape off her hands, eyes, and mouth. She didn't know where she was, but she could see a light down the road. She was on a blacktop highway. The lights from a house not far off the road beckoned her.

The man of the house answered the door and saw Emily, who had burst into tears. His wife walked in from the other room and looked with shock at the disheveled mess standing in the entry.

"Please, call 9–1–1." Emily, in tears, tried to scream but could only gasp, "I was kidnapped."

The woman of the house wrapped a blanket around their frightened young visitor and they soon heard sirens nearing the house. Emily's moans and cries filled the room as questions flew at her. Trying to gather her wits, she asked for time to collect her thoughts. The deputies who had responded agreed to give her time to compose herself; but they didn't want her to forget what had happened. Every detail she could recall would give them a better chance at catching the kidnapper.

The deputies gently put Emily into the back of their squad car. The ride to the sheriff's office was short, and Emily was soon drinking a cup of hot coffee. The sheriff knew who she was and where she was staying. He immediately called Billie. She and Stone were quickly on their way to the office.

Emily cried when she saw them. Stone was the first to walk in the door. Hugging her tightly, he felt her body quivering as she sobbed on his shoulder. Emily still had the warm blanket draped over her, and Stone wrapped it even tighter as he helped her into the back seat of the car. Billie sat in the back seat, holding her hand as they traveled back to the resort.

"You *will* stay at the lodge tonight," Billie said. Emily nodded in agreement.

CHAPTER 21

"I'M HURTING"

———◆———

WHEN EMILY OPENED HER EYES, it took her a couple seconds to realize where she was and what had happened. The room at the lodge was comfortable and familiar; she had stayed with Jenny many times and had slept in most of the rooms at one time or another. Her other waking memory gave her a start—a creepy, frightened feeling that held her in its grip but ended when she assured herself she was safe; but what an ordeal she had lived through. She knew there were others who had not lived to escape and tell.

The sheriff had told Emily he'd be out in the morning to take a statement. Hopefully her memory would be clear and her fear a bit more under control. At the station, she hardly knew her own name. He wanted to give her a chance to feel safe; the ordeal was over.

Emily walked to the end of the floor to shower. When she walked by the storage room on the left, a sense of anguish surged through her body. She stopped for a second and was about to open the door when a feeling of intense sorrow flowed through her mind. She hurriedly found her way to the shower. The warm water cascaded over her and she was calmed.

Billie had a huge breakfast ready, and Stone brought her a cup of coffee. Asking how her night had been, they told her the sheriff had called to say he would be out within the hour. As she ate, she told them about the sensation she had when she walked by the last door.

"You and Jenny used to play in that room—Josh, too. It had cable TV when not all the rooms did. You three loved to watch music videos and dance."

"That's funny," Emily said, "I don't remember anything about that— only the strange feeling I had now when I walked by."

Sheriff Emerson knocked on the door, and Billie invited him in. Kirsten, working the switchboard, would love to have listened in on the conversation between Emerson and Emily. However, she knew she would have to wait until the next meeting of the law enforcement agencies and BCA before she would find out anything.

Emily dreaded the questions he would ask, having to relive her kidnapping. They went into the living room and sat down. Billie closed the French doors so they would have privacy. Emerson was kind and gentle in his questioning. He told her he was recording her account of the abduction and also taking notes. While the questions were quite basic, he was careful not to generate more angst; Emily was uneasy and frightened enough as it was. He did, however, ask at one point if Emily was sure both were men. Her description of the one perpetrator—soft spoken and supple hands made the sheriff wonder.

Emily told of the strong arm around her neck, of waking in what she thought was a large warehouse, and of the two people and their conversations. Occasionally horror overcame her. She would cry, compose herself, and then go on with her story.

She seemed to have meticulous memories of every detail; the sheriff had to ask few questions. As the story of killers and fetishes flowed, Emily's strength of character emerged. Sheriff Emerson could not help but wonder about this articulate, brave woman sitting next to him. Years ago she had been suspected of hiding information about a homicide.

The interrogation ended, and Billie had cups of strong coffee and cinnamon rolls for each of them. Emily felt spent and told Billie she was ready to go back to her cabin. She may come back to spend the night at the lodge, but for now, a nap and the quiet of her own place was calling her. Emily collapsed on the old worn couch as soon as she walked through the door and was soon asleep.

Sheriff Emerson called Kirsten at the resort. "I can't believe Emily knows anything about Jenny's death. She's a tough nut, and I don't think she'd keep that inside, unless of course she knows something but truly doesn't remember." He went on to say that he knows people change, that she could have been trouble years ago, but nothing pointed to that. He liked her tenacity and her determination to move forward and not be intimidated by her abduction. Her kidnappers were not going to control her life.

Emily awoke when Billie knocked on her door. She had been determined not to let her fear have power over her and had spent the day resting in her cabin.

"Supper is ready," Billie said. "I'll walk with you to the lodge."

Shane had noticed that Emily's car wasn't home when he awoke in the middle of the night. He hugged her after walking in with Billie. He had called his home office and told them he had an emergency delaying his return from Hidden Rapids. He had been beating himself up for failing to protect her.

Shane had to return to work in Minneapolis but he called Emily every evening, and soon she was telling him about her returning to California.

Because of her determination, Emily's life returned to normalcy somewhat quickly. She would soon be back to taking care of her responsibilities in California. Night sweats occasionally woke her when panic washed over her. Getting up for a while and reassuring herself she was safe helped her through the fear. Billie had asked her to stay on and decorate the older cabins. Instead, she agreed to come back after finishing her project in California. She sensed that she had unfinished business in this area, although she couldn't put a finger on exactly what it was.

The newspaper had kept her name and the exact details of her kidnapping under wraps. The townspeople knew there had been an attack, but that was all. Law enforcement hoped someone would come forward with information about that night. Perhaps they had seen something or someone acting suspicious the night of the reunion at the fairgrounds. Stone's name had come up as had Shane's. Stone had been with Kirsten during the entire night of the reunion at the fairgrounds except for her brief time in the restroom. Shane had returned to the resort before Emily and Stone had talked. It had been a brief exchange, and Stone and Kirsten were on their way home, as was Emily.

CHAPTER 22

"THE MOTHER AND CHILD REUNION"

———◆———

BILLIE MADE CALLS TO ARRANGE a coffee party for Roxanne and Holly before Emily's departure. Holly had reluctantly agreed to come. Emily and Holly were just a couple years apart. Emily had graduated with Eric, and Holly had married Emily's brother Josh.

Roxanne was feeling nervous so Billie helped her with her clothes and hair. They had shopped the week before to get a few summer tops, shorts, a sundress, and sandals. Roxanne was careful not to bring too much into the little cabin.

Sessions with her therapist were long and arduous. Remembering the heartache and sorrow that had been such a part of her life left her thoughts tangled and her mind hurting. Roxanne felt it was too painful to reflect on her sadness for very long. She had learned to rescue herself from too much grief.

As Holly drove up, Roxanne's anxiety heightened. She had not seen her daughter in so long. She watched Holly get out of the car and was reminded how attractive she was. Holly looked like a young version of her mom. Billie greeted Holly with a hug. Roxanne moved from behind the kitchen door, walking out with as much confidence as she could muster. Tears streamed down Holly's face as she wrapped her arms around her mother.

"You look wonderful, Mom. How do you feel?" Holly looked deeply into her mother's eyes and saw the mother she had known when she was young.

"I'm doing really well," Roxanne replied, her voice soft and hesitant. "I now see a therapist in Hidden Rapids three times a week, and I'm working hard on my problems. I want to beat this thing."

Emily walked in just as the emotional meeting was ending. She too hugged Holly and was glad to see her. She had made up her mind not to talk about Josh. Holly did not deserve to be placed in the middle of sibling contention.

Billie served hot banana nut muffins complemented with hazelnut flavored coffee. The four women found a variety of subjects to chat about; the morning passed quickly. Holly and Roxanne made plans to meet for lunch; Emily and Holly would find another time to talk again soon.

Roxanne thanked Billie for the lovely coffee party and returned to her cabin. The house plan book was a fascination, and she settled into a chair with plans in hand. She looked carefully through each page. Drawings of house exteriors and layouts of interiors were captivating. She reminded herself she could have anything she wanted; Barry could build her *anything.*

Roxanne thought she might wear the pages out as she thumbed through the book over and over. She had liked the plan that Barry had shown her for his spec house. It had flowed comfortably from one room to another; however, it was a bit small for her. She would need a large house. There were three grandchildren who might stay overnight sometimes to swim and water ski for hours. *It could happen* she told herself. *I could get better. I could win the battle against this demon.*

Roxanne let her dream of family drift along. She could picture her daughter, stopping by just to visit over a quick cup of coffee on her way to work; or attending her grandchildren's school functions; or being a part of their birthdays and holidays; or Christmas together. She sobbed as she thought of being reunited with her family. She slipped a piece of paper into the plan book to mark the house Barry would build.

Emily drove to Northern Exposure to tell her father of her plan to be back in the area as soon as her commitments in California were done. Lucy was in his apartment when she arrived but left immediately. "She thinks you don't like her," her father said with sadness.

"I *don't* like her," Emily quickly replied. "Why would I? The two of you have had an ongoing affair—for years. My mother knew about it. Gambling is an illness, Dad. You should have been there for Mom, helping her instead of running around with Lucy." Emily's voice grew louder with each sentence. She was screaming now, and crying. "The whole town knew. How do you think Josh and I felt?"

A knock on the door startled the two and a voice with authority asked if things were all right. "Paul," a male voice asked, "are you okay? It's a little noisy in there."

"Yes," Paul hurriedly answered, "We're fine."

"Okay," the man answered, "but let's keep it down."

Paul walked quickly over to Emily and put his arms around her. "I am so sorry. I didn't do the right thing for my family. Please forgive me."

Emily collapsed into a chair and regained control. She wiped her tears and told her father of her plans to return to Hidden Rapids after concluding her decorating commitment in California. She would come back for a few weeks, maybe a month or so, to redecorate some of the older cabins at Stonebridge. She also asked about their family cabin. Did he want to sell it to Billie and the resort? They hadn't talked about it, but she was sure they would be interested.

Paul didn't know how to reply. He wanted to get Emily's thoughts before making a decision. He knew Josh didn't care what was done with the cabin. Paul did remark about the cost to upgrade and the fact that it sat right in the middle of Stonebridge. Neither the guests at the resort or the Blake's had privacy. Emily loved that old cabin but had to agree there were few reasons to continue ownership. They agreed they would sell it.

Paul decided to call and set up a meeting with Billie. He called right away and told her of their discussion. He didn't want her thinking they were coming for coffee and a visit. He wanted to give her a chance to think about it, talk to Stone, and probably contact their attorney. Paul and Emily were sure that Billie would jump at the chance to have their little bird's nest. That's the name they had given it when it was built. It was small but cozy and perfect for the four of them.

Arrangements were made to come to the lodge the next morning. Paul had invited Josh to join them, but he had declined. Billie and Stone were all smiles as they welcomed Emily and Paul. The aroma of an egg bake and blueberry muffins made their stomachs growl. Paul began the discussion. He had contacted a realtor and had a price in mind. As they enjoyed breakfast on the deck, the beauty of the lake and nostalgic thoughts soared through Emily and Paul's minds. Giving up this piece of heaven would be difficult. Emily could not stop the tear that rolled so quietly down her cheek. Her father reached for her hand and took a long deep breath.

Billie had known the difficulty they would have in giving up the place where so many memories had been made. They would still, however, have the recollections; and she had a better offer for them. She and Stone had talked about the best price to offer them for the property and, more specifically, how they could help them feel good about the decision to sell. They were well aware of the pain Emily and Paul would feel about selling their place.

Billie got up from the table and walked over to Paul. Standing behind him, she placed her hands on his shoulders. He had been the love of her dear friend Charlotte and always special to her. However, his property sitting in the middle of the resort, while not a huge problem, had become a bone of contention and had impacted their friendship.

"We have an offer for you that would enable you to continue living next to the water," Billie said with a jovial tone. "We'll trade the chalet at the end of the resort for yours. The place is new and not quite finished. With Emily's decorating skills, it would be a perfect retreat. It will give us both what we want. You'll still have the memories of the cabin, and you won't have to give up the splendor of Pokegama."

Time for smiles and hugs had left the food to cool and the coffee needing a minute in the microwave. What had begun as a sad day had become a day to celebrate. Papers would be signed in the next week, and Emily would handle the finishing touches on their new vacation villa. Paint and floor covering was yet to be chosen, and Emily was already mentally redoing the cabins at Stonebridge.

CHAPTER 23

"It's Such A Pretty World Today"

THE CONTRACTOR WAS ALL SET to start the house for Roxanne, and Roxanne was ready for her new life. Barry had done the detail work. There was a time when he would list the materials, starting with the sill plate and working up from there. These days, a computer read the plan and listed the materials for him: the lumber to shell up the structure, windows, doors, insulation, sheetrock, right down to the pounds of nails and fasteners needed.

The basement had been dug, which was immediately followed by a week's rain. So the contractor continued his finishing work on a home in town and waited for the rain to subside. The site where Roxanne's house would be built was close to the old one. Debris from the fire had been hauled away, and the area had been filled with flowers and trees. The sandy soil dried quickly, so soon the basement was completed. Jack brought her to the building site almost every afternoon. They often stopped at Zorbaz on their way back to Jack's. Roxanne had given in to Jack and Billie's urging and moved into the apartment over Jack's boathouse. Although they saw each other often, Jack still had a full work schedule and his days were busy. Roxanne's days were also full with therapy three days a week and helping Billie at the resort whenever possible.

Her apartment was sparse but neat and clean. She struggled every day to keep it that way. She read the newspaper at Billie's. It was in the lodge for customers to enjoy. Every morning Roxanne would place yesterday's paper in the recycle bin. At times, it was a struggle, a battle, to resist taking it home, to read it just one more time, to clip parts of it for later information, she told herself.

Magazines also lay in the recycle bin and boxes. She might need those when she moved. The conflict going on in her mind was a fierce one. She feared she had a split personality. One part of her was confident and trustworthy, knowing what she was up against and ready for the challenge. The other part was clingy and frightened. Her *things* had been her comfort, and now most of the *things* that surrounded her belonged to someone else. Jack and Billie provided her with the necessities of life. Jack's apartment had everything she needed. She brought her laundry to the resort and took care of that chore while she helped Billie.

It was comforting for Roxanne to be back with her dear friend. Billie had good days and also some extremely bad ones. She would be working when, all of a sudden, she would feel weak and dizzy and often fainted. Roxanne was needed and had begun to believe she did deserve a place in this world—a reason to live.

Roxanne had been thinking about buying a vehicle for a few weeks. It had been a long time since she had been behind the wheel of a car, but she had kept her driver's license current and decided she would ask Jack if he would take her to a dealership to see about a purchase.

After their usual check on her house, she brought up the subject. Jack did not hesitate, and that made her feel good. "Of course you should have a car," he said. "I'll help you get your driving skills back." He reached over and squeezed her hand as he spoke. He gave her a short hug often but had been careful not to expect affection returned. He steadied her thoughts and actions with his presence. *Why didn't I marry him?* she wondered.

The car salesman welcomed the customers. He was new to the dealership, so he did not know them. Jack had lived there so long he normally knew every person no matter where they worked downtown. The young man assumed they were married and referred to them as husband and wife. Roxanne was a bit embarrassed, but Jack handled it well. Roxanne spotted a tan sedan she liked. It didn't take her long to say she would take it, but they would have to deliver it. The look on the young sales-man's face was priceless. Before he could answer, Jack assured Roxanne he would arrange to get it home and the lessons would begin that night.

Roxanne was feeling smug as they drove home. She was proud of her choice and the way she had handled the purchase. She didn't have to take hours or even days to decide. Normally, *any* decision was wrenching and consequently nothing would get done.

She was a perfectionist and knew perfectionists were particularly vulnerable to getting caught up in hoarding. She was certainly aware of her compulsive personality. Though she had seemed confident when she was younger, she had hidden her insecurities and was often caught up in self-doubt. Roxanne had made a large decision, and she was elat-ed. Her confidence soared.

Barry walked her through the many decisions needed for new con-struction. Emily would help select the windows, doors, cabinets, showers, toilets, and vanities. They would take it slow, giving Roxanne a maximum of three choices. The three of them had discussed all of this at great length before the project was started. There were ground rules with a promise either to adhere to them or to halt the process immediately.

Paint and decorating would be totally Emily's job, and she would not even discuss it with Roxanne until the house was built. Too many deci-sions for Roxanne would be counterproductive, making her mind reel and plunge into trepidation.

Jack was giving her daily driving lessons, and she was getting reac-quainted with her home area. Driving must be like riding a bike she had decided, because it came right back to her. Her skills on parking and driving in traffic needed work, but her confidence was growing.

South Hwy.169 led them to the sign pointing to Sugar Hills Lodge. They loved the restaurant and savored a delicious dinner, soaking up the splendor of turquoise-colored Sugar Lake and surroundings, and the glorious summer sunset. How she had been willing to give this all up was a mystery.

Continued therapy gave Roxanne confidence and motivation to get better, to conquer the demons that had ruled her mind for so long. Her therapist encouraged Roxanne to grieve—to dare to feel the hurt and to embrace her love for her son Eric and for her parents.

"Grief is as old as mankind," her therapist reminded her. "However, it is also the most neglected emotion." She went on to tell Roxanne that this neglect had come at an enormous cost to her. Roxanne's repressed grief had kept her in a continued state of stress and shock.

Roxanne had been given homework and reading to help her stay focused on the real problem. She was fortunate to have several people in her life that she could talk to. Holly and Jack were quite supportive, but Billie was the go-to person. She was there any time of the day or night and always ready to listen.

Roxanne's therapist would always remind her, "You can postpone grief, but you cannot avoid it." Roxanne would experience wrenching pain, physical pain that would make her double over. Her body was finally reacting to the sorrow she had suppressed for so long. Grief-caused pain that sunk into her very bones would leave Roxanne exhausted. Those days at first were terribly depressing, her body feeling worn out, like she had just been beaten.

CHAPTER 24

"California Bound"

———➤———

EMILY PACKED ONLY A FEW things as most of her clothes were still in California. She drove to Duluth in the afternoon, having made a reservation at The Inn on the Lake for the night.

Her flight left in the morning. She returned her rental car, would enjoy breakfast at Grandma's Restaurant, and take a cab to the airport in the morning. Perfect sunny weather and the smell of Lake Superior beckoned her to enjoy the waterfront walk. Ships slowly worked their way to the lift bridge. Emily had enjoyed shopping and watching the bridge open to let the cumbersome vessels through when she was younger, but this was like a new experience.

Emily had slept like a baby in the comfort of the fabulous hotel, feeling as if she had not a care in the world. She couldn't even explain her lack of concern. There was still a mountain of unfinished business in Hidden Rapids, and there was the fright during and following her abduction; but she seemed to be able to set that aside, at least for now. The reality that her abductor had not been caught loomed large in her mind at times, but leaving Hidden Rapids seemed to quell that worry.

After a shower the next morning and packing her suitcase, she walked over to Grandma's for a quick breakfast. It had been a long time since she had enjoyed a tasty meal there, and it did not disappoint her. Four women sat at the table next to her. They were tastefully dressed, and Emily could hear enough of the conversation, though some of it was

Blood Moon

hush-hush, to know they were smart professional women. Every one of them was attractive, but the lady in the lime green sweater was exceptionally beautiful.

Emily envied the four friends as they laughed and talked. She suddenly felt sad she had lost contact with her high school and college friends. It was her doing. When she graduated and moved to California, she was so committed to making a name for herself in the decorating business that she let her personal life suffer. She discreetly took a picture of the foursome to remind herself of what she had missed...much as one would snap a picture of a great haircut to try some day.

Chantal sipped her latté as she, a prosecutor, and two women from the Minnesota Bureau of Criminal Apprehension ate their breakfasts. They had all been college friends and had found positions in the area. They gathered once a month to talk, laugh, and lighten their lives. Stress and pressure from their careers brought pride in their accomplishments but also anxiety. They had each broken the glass ceiling.

Their visits were about their occupations but also the usual girl talk. One of the women lowered her voice when she spoke of the kidnapping of a 40-year-old woman in Hidden Rapids. She told some of the details of the crime, the bizarre manicure and pedicure. Chantal had heard from one of the deputies of St. Louis County about the abduction but had no details.

"There may be two perps involved," April from the BCA rather whispered raising her eyebrows. "It sounds like there could be two—each with a nail polish fetish."

Breakfast and lively discussion ended, and Chantal returned to the courthouse. It was Tuesday and the morning had already been busy. She had been wiped out when she returned home the day before. Mondays were always busy as that was the day she met with the attorneys. That day would decide if there would be plea bargains or a trial. Chantal had been too tired to think about the kidnapping of the woman from Hidden Rapids.

125

Tuesday morning she pulled her light blue blouse collar up and slipped her black garb on. Smoothing the collar against the black robe she told the bailiff she was ready.

"All rise." The voice of the bailiff quieted the people in the court-room. "The Honorable Chantal McAllister presiding."

Kyle Jenkins stood before her this drizzly morning while his attor-ney pleaded for another chance for his client. The next step should be incarceration, but she could be lenient and not send this bum to jail. Judge McAllister had no compassion. She read aloud his offense and his sentence. "Offense July 2, 2015. Felony: Second degree drugs, sale 3 grams or more, cocaine/heroin/meth within 90-day period; commit to commissioner of corrections, 78 months; supply DNA sample."

The day continued. Chantal sentenced criminals and felt no remorse for her harsh rulings. She adhered to the letter of the law keeping with the guidelines set up by the court.

With the docket completed for the day, Chantal drove home. She was tired. After pouring a glass of Merlot and putting a few pretzels in a bowl, she settled in and fired up her computer. There were many emails. She clicked on the top one: *2_hot_4_u_Jessie.*

Thoughts of April's comment invaded her mind, and she had trou-ble concentrating on the intriguing emails. Chantal stopped thinking of the person she had met on the Internet the minute their encounter ended. It may be that she took the initiative and was the power broker. She may or may not drug him and abscond with his money and credit cards, but sometimes she simply wanted—needed—a man's attention and took pleasure in sex.

The comments about a nail fetish unnerved her. She had been with that goofball from Hidden Rapids awhile ago. He could be involved in the kidnapping. She got up and paced around the den. Chantal was known as Judge Judy of the North Country. She could feel a roaring headache coming on as she recalled her reputation as a no nonsense judge. She smiled slyly as she thought to herself, *but I like a little nonsense.*

The phone number for silent witness scrolled through her brain. She had often repeated that number to defendants who had told her they had found themselves caught up in situations they could not get out of. "Make a call," she would say with a harsh tone in her voice. "Don't play the part of a victim trapped in a criminal act. You can always get out if you want to."

She sighed and put her swimsuit and cover-up on. Grabbing a towel, she made her way to the elevator and descended to the fourth floor. A warm pool and later the hot tub relieved her aching head and settled her down. The stress left and she made her way back to her condo, went to bed, and quickly fell asleep.

It took strong coffee and a good dose of Good Morning, America to clear her head. The name of Chantal's prey flooded her thoughts: "Brian Abbott" had leaped off the face of the credit card she had stolen and sold. He was a risk-taker and had an absolute obsession for nail polish. She could still picture the polish lined up on the table in the tent on Sugar Lake. She hadn't given it much thought until now. Most of the men she had become involved with had some kind of a fetish. Chantal had her own obsession—she liked men, money, and sex. Not necessarily in that order.

She believed she was an excellent judge; perhaps even to call herself remarkable was not overstating her ability. Chantal saw herself as an umpire—a referee—for those who could not handle life.

Searching the Internet to see who and what Brian Abbott was gave her an excellent look into his life. He owned a bank, was married, had no children, and had been a popular sports figure in high school and college. He was bright, had attended a reputable college, and, over time, had contributed a great deal of money and time to the betterment of Hidden Rapids.

"Well, maybe he has his good points, she thought.

As the week came to an end, Chantal thought more and more about the kidnapped woman. She asked herself over and over if the man she had met could be involved. She had a good life now—a profession that she was born for—and she would do nothing to jeopardize her career.

The adjustment had been difficult. No, *difficult* was not a strong enough word. The change had been more than just life altering. It had been the passing away of a young girl and the reawakening of a young woman. Chantal's thoughts turned to her mother, the woman she had called mom for 18 years. Her mother had thought their lives were ideal. There was always money, and therefore the material possessions of everyday life were plentiful. Her mother could not—would not—believe that the men who came through their home, entering and exiting through what seemed like their revolving door, stayed around at least long enough to molest her child.

Sometimes it was the faces of those men she saw in her escapades with lovers she met on line. Brian had been one of those, a man who seemed to come out of her past. Actually as she thought of him, he should be glad she didn't really hurt him. She could have given him a much bigger dose of the knockout drug. He could have been out of it for hours, maybe even days, and lost some of his memory forever.

"Yes," she said, now speaking out loud. "I could have screwed up his life for a long time—maybe forever. I went easy on him."

She thought of her mother again. Chantal hated when those thoughts arrived. She had long ago decided her mother was out of her life. She couldn't believe that the police weren't after her when she first went missing and that at the very least it would have been on the news with her picture blasted across the TV and on posters stapled on poles around the neighborhood.

As the reflection of her actions years ago came into her mind, she remembered the extensive consideration she had given toward her own disappearance. A trust fund, set up by her father, became available when she turned 18. She had emptied the account that very day. She left with her latest boyfriend who had friends in Minnesota. Their romance hadn't last long, but she had found close friends in the apartment she had rented in St. Paul.

Since money was not a problem, she had enrolled at the University of Minnesota and later William Mitchell Law School. Her given full name was long because her mother thought it looked impressive to have several names. Her name-change decision had been uncomplicated. Her high school diploma had listed so many names that she simply went to a judge and asked to change her name legally to one first, middle, and last. Once the judge saw the names Christina Annette Darla Chantal McAllister Sutton Fitzgerald on her birth certificate and high school diploma, he just smiled and quietly asked her which names she preferred. She had chosen Chantal Annette McAllister and never looked back.

She had gone to great lengths never to be found; yet she was somewhat disappointed that no one had come looking for her. She didn't feel valued—not even important enough for her mom to search for her.

Her brief feelings of rejection left, and she went on with the business of the day. Chantal had made many friends; some were close, and she knew she could rely on them. She dated, though never let anyone get too significant. If she began to feel too close to them, she ended the relationship with hardly a notice. Many thought she was a lesbian, and that was also fine with her. Chantal had too many skeletons in her closet; and other than brief intimate sessions with strangers, she was only accountable to herself.

Duluth had been good to her. She had spent the only enjoyable time of her life in the Seaport City visiting her grandparents. When she graduated with a law degree, the only place that she could think of to go was Duluth. Although her grandparents had passed away, the memories of the idyllic life she remembered while vacationing there drew her in. The city offered the opportunities of a large city but the sense of a small town.

Three other women from her college days had also found their way to the shores of majestic Lake Superior. Considered by most to be the largest body of fresh-water lake in the world, tourists flocked to the grand body of water to vacation in all the seasons. At one time, Duluth was supposedly home to more millionaires per capita than anywhere else in the United States.

The extraordinary Congdon mansion, called Glensheen, was a place Chantal often took her visiting friends and colleagues. The infamous murders in 1977 made headlines around the United States. Elizabeth Congdon was suffocated with a satin pillow in her sister Helen's bedroom; and her nurse, Velma Pietila, was found lying on a window seat, beaten to death with a candle stick.

Elizabeth's son-in-law, Roger Caldwell, was eventually charged and convicted of the murders in 1978. The Minnesota Supreme Court overturned Roger's conviction in 1983. He accepted a plea deal, a confession to second-degree murder and time served. He committed suicide in 1988.

Chantal was captivated by the story. The dark side of human behavior fascinated her.

CHAPTER 25

"LIVING THE LIE"

———

AFTER BREAKFAST, EMILY WAS ON the plane to Minneapolis where she would board Delta Airlines for her trip to California. She had a lengthy layover in Minneapolis but enjoyed her time in the airport relaxing and reading a good book.

The hustle of LAX airport had not changed. She hailed a cab and was soon had her on her way back to her condo. She had not been gone all that long, but it felt like an eternity. Life for her had changed.

Shane. She thought of him and smiled. Her renewed friendship with him pleased her. The all-class reunion had gone remarkably well, and some of the anxiety she had felt over facing her past hadn't amounted to anything. One brief moment with the jerk, Scott Turner, had worried her, but with Shane's help, her discomfort had been short-lived. The terror she had experienced at the hands of two torturers and would-be killers had definitely given her a lasting lesson on what's important, what really matters and what is trivial in life.

She and Shane spoke often. They used cell phones, email, and Facebook to keep in touch with each other. They were both feeling a close bond, and Emily loved the way she was beginning to experience a perhaps lasting love.

Rebel welcomed her home with constant meowing. The neighbor had taken good care of the spoiled feline, but Rebel was glad to have his mistress home. He wound himself around her legs and settled next to her on the sofa.

Emily was awake early the next morning and anxious to get this decorating project finished. She called the cranky, has-been actress and was soon on her way to the mansion on the hill. The cook offered her freshly squeezed orange juice, coffee, and cranberry muffins. Sybil waltzed into the dining room, wearing a long white dress and wrapped in a bright blue shawl. "Let's sit outside in the sunshine while we talk about the changes I want to make."

"Changes?" Emily's tone was suddenly brusque. "I thought we had decided on everything—that you had okayed everything," she said, her tone still curt.

"They're minor," the owner said with a smile and a pat on Emily's shoulder.

For some reason, the woman was chatty and even friendly as she herself poured Emily a cup of chocolate mint coffee. Sybil talked of the news she had heard on Good Morning America, and the sunny weather California was experiencing while much of the northeast was getting a cold blast. It was girl talk—so unlike other conversations they had had.

Sybil seemed genuinely interested in Emily's personal life today and of course knew she had been away for a time. When Emily told her she had been in Hidden Rapids, Minnesota, the old woman's eyes lit up. "I'm originally from Duluth," she said with a gleam in her eye.

She spilled out her life story with the drama of a charmed life on the coast of Lake Superior and a surreptitious love affair with a married businessman—a close friend of her father's. She had left for the bright lights of Hollywood and had become a mediocre actress. The estrangement with her parents had ended with the birth of her daughter Tina and her returns to Duluth for regular visits.

As Sybil's tale continued, a handsome young man came from around the corner of the pool house, kissed Sybil on the cheek, and reminded her of their golf date and luncheon later. "He's a bit younger," she said with a huge smile on her lips, "but he is interested in me, and I find him fascinating."

Emily now understood her elderly client's cheerful mood. She had a gigolo. Rita, Sybil's personal assistant, joined them for a few minutes with some paperwork for Sybil to sign. The disgusted look she gave Rex let Emily know that Rita did *not* favor the relationship.

Their chatting continued. Sybil made a few minor changes in the color of some of the accessories and accents in the décor; but they were inconsequential, and Emily relaxed. She wondered how the woman she was sitting with was going to protect herself from the handsome con man. Rex Martin, tanned and muscular, came across as a good-looking attentive guy. Emily felt sorry for Sybil as she watched him romance her.

Emily would need several appointments with Sybil, and they were still making decisions on a few fabrics and shades of color for the great room. Sybil wanted a mix of traditional and modern. She liked clean lines but would also want to throw in a funky antique.

The den would look vintage Hollywood. The upholstered furniture would be damask, lace, and a bit of floral. A rock fireplace was the focal point of the room. As Emily and Sybil walked in to re-measure the room and talk about material, Emily's eye again caught the elegant picture on the wall. The portrait of a stunningly gorgeous young woman in a large silver and black ornate frame looked down on them. Her eyes had a yearning in them, and her lips bore no smile.

"Your daughter is so beautiful." Emily said.

"Yes, she was," Sybil replied, accenting the word *was.*"

"Are the authorities still looking for her?" Emily asked. She instantly wished she had worded it differently.

"No," Sybil answered quickly. "They never looked very hard. She went missing—dead—I'm quite sure," Sybil spoke in a barely audible voice.

"I'm so sorry," Emily quickly replied wishing she had not even asked about the young woman.

"Tina was unhappy here—unhappy with me—and left when she turned 18. She left one morning and never returned. I myself believe one of the young men she was involved with killed her."

It was absolutely time for Emily to take her leave. She told Sybil she would call her the next day and left. The picture of Tina lingered in her mind as she drove down the long winding driveway. She felt sad for Sybil. She was so alone. Well, not quite alone. She had Rex.

Emily settled in to look over the pictures she had taken of the mansion. The outside was mostly finished, and the inside was taking shape nicely. She came to the picture of the large fireplace with Tina's portrait hanging above it. As she stared at the image of the striking young woman, she sensed she may have seen her before. Reading a bit before bed, Emily began to think hard about where they might have encountered each other, but that was impossible. She soon fell asleep.

Emily awoke with a start in the middle of the night. She may have seen the woman in Duluth at Grandma's Restaurant. She quickly thumbed through the pictures on her phone, and there it was—a picture of the four women having lunch together. The one in the green sweater could be the woman in the portrait. She expanded the photo on the screen and looked long and hard at it. "Yes!" she said loudly, alarming Rebel enough to jump off the bed and scamper away.

Okay, she had settled down now and knew it seemed preposterous. Tina could not possibly be the woman she saw eating with her friends in Duluth. Emily was too busy even to think about Tina—or the fact that the woman in Duluth had an uncanny resemblance to the portrait hanging over Sybil's fireplace. Emily's days were full of drapery decisions and furniture placements. Dining room table and chairs had arrived; and white wicker furniture had turned the sunroom into a charming gathering area.

Sybil was pleased and already planning the parties she and Rex would host. Guest lists were long and included many of the old Hollywood actors and actresses. Their glory days had passed, but love for their craft and each other had not.

Shane flew out for a weekend get-a-way, and Emily was excited to pick him up at the airport. They had a weekend of site seeing planned. The weather was warm and sunny, and the Pacific Coast Highway was magnificent. They stayed at the Castle Inn outside of Cambria. Elephant seals rested on the white sand below the boardwalk. The giants were sedentary except for an occasional movement to throw sand onto their bodies.

Emily and Shane felt close. Their slow easy relationship was beginning to include each other more and more. Hours of reminiscing about their lives in Hidden Rapids and their mutual friends had bound them even closer. Long talks on the phone and constant texts brought them comfort neither had experienced before. Besides a sense of falling leisurely in love, they were true friends. They shared hopes and dreams for their future. Laughter was a distinct part of their relationship, and the simplicity with which the two complemented the other in actions and thoughts was undeniable. Shane had felt horrible remorse over leaving Emily at the class reunion. Even though she had insisted on driving separately, he believed he should have stayed with her until she was safely in the car. Emily had been extremely resilient, even laughing at times at the behavior of the abductors. The experience had been creepy and yet comical, all at the same time.

Emily took Shane past the driveway of the house she had been working on. She did not think it proper to drive down the secluded lane but told him all about it as she slowly passed the property. When they were having lunch, she showed him the cell phone pictures of the rooms that she had totally redone. As he scrolled through photos, he came to the one she had taken in Duluth of the four women having lunch.

"How do you know April?" he asked, pointing to one of the women in the picture.

"You *know* one of them?" Emily was surprised and excited.

"Yes," Shane laughed and nodded his head. "She's April Butler. April works for the BCA. I see her all the time."

"Do you know the others?" Emily's breathing quickened. She felt ecstatic.

"Jane works for the BCA, too," he said, pointing his finger at the blond-haired woman taking a bite of her sandwich. "I know the judge, too: Chantal McAllister. She's better known as The Hanging Judge. She doesn't really hang anyone, but she is tough on criminals. Her Honor always gives the longest sentences allowed. I don't know her well but have been to some conferences with her and several parties."

Emily grabbed the phone out of his hand and scrolled back to the pictures in Sybil's home. Finding the shot of Tina's portrait, she showed it to Shane and asked if it could be the same woman. He studied the young woman's face carefully, then went back to the four sitting at Grandma's Café. He was amazed. They did look a lot alike. Studying facial features and bone structure was his expertise. He thought they could indeed be the same woman. He told Emily he would check things out as soon as he was back in Minnesota.

Shane had only been able to take a short amount of time off from work, and soon Emily was dropping him off at LAX. Their time together had been amazing, and they each wanted more of the other.

Emily drove back to Hidden Rapids after another ten days of tying up loose ends. She wanted her car in Hidden Rapids but kept her apartment in California. It was still a mystery where her home would eventually be. Rebel had joined his mistress for this trip. She hoped he would adjust to living at the lake.

Shane had been home only a few days when a chance came for him to ask April about Chantal. April had come to the home office in Minneapolis to check in with her superiors on a case she was working. Shane asked what she knew about Chantal's background.

April shrugged her shoulders and laughed. "No one knows anything about Chantal's past. She doesn't share anything about her life before we all met in college. We're good friends. I like her and would trust her with my life, but she's not giving anyone an *in* to her history."

Shane found the picture in his phone that Emily had forwarded to him.

April took a long hard look at it, enlarged it, and looked for an extended time at the face of the beautiful woman. "It could be her," she said, "but I can't be sure."

Shane went on to explain who she might be and why he even knew anything about the situation.

"Forward the picture to me," April said, with a flippant tone in her voice. "I'll just ask her."

Shane sent the photo with Emily's number, in case Chantal had questions. He knew it was a long shot, but at least he could tell Emily he tried.

CHAPTER 26

"NEW DAY"

———◆———

APRIL DIDN'T WASTE ANY TIME getting Chantal on the phone. "Let's meet for a cocktail and dinner at the Radisson after work," she said with not a hint of the real reason for her wanting to connect. Shane had forwarded the picture to her, and she had studied it for a long time. "Yes," she said to herself, "it certainly could be Chantal." She had long teased her friend about the secrecy in her past. Chantal had always guarded her privacy, and her friends had become accustomed to the mystery she maintained. Many believed it was just her way of trying to protect her anonymity. She was a prominent judge who was often in the news; many of her cases were high profile.

Chantal had already arrived and found a table close to the door. She had positioned herself with her back to the wall, able to see all around the room. April knew Chantal carried a gun with her at all times and was skilled in the use of it. The judge's life had occasionally been threatened, and she had developed proficiency in self-protection.

April ordered a glass of chardonnay. Chantal already had a martini in front of her. April took her phone out, found the picture, and proceeded to place it in front of her unsuspecting friend.

"Is this you?" April asked as she put the picture in front of Chantal's face. There was no drama in her voice; it was just a matter-of-fact question.

The pretty young woman pictured in the silver and black frame looked back at Chantal. She took a long, concerted breath, intending to deny with fervor that the portrait was of her. Instead, she replied with a sigh and a tear, "Yes—yes, it is."

April was speechless, partly because of the admission but mostly because of the tear that fell slowly down her friend's cheek. There was an uncomfortable silence, then the slow painstaking story of Chantal's childhood. April sat spellbound by the narrative. She sat silent, hardly breathing as Chantal told of the abuse by her mother's boyfriends and her seeming non-existence in her mother's life.

When the chronicle was finished, Chantal ordered a steak, baked potato with sour cream and butter, and a Caesar salad. April ordered a full meal also and then handed Chantal a piece of paper with Emily's phone number on it.

"You can call her for more information if you like," April said as they ate their salads. "Emily is decorating your mother's house. That's how the picture came to be noticed. Emily was en route from Hidden Rapids to Los Angeles and flew out of Duluth into Minneapolis," April explained. She went on to tell about Emily taking their picture while they ate at Grandma's just because they represented what she had missed with her friends from school.

"The picture in your mom's house caught her eye, and Emily's a friend of Shane Powell. She was showing him the pictures of her latest decorating job when he recognized you." April was talking fast now and nervously trying to explain how this dark secret came into the light.

The judge seemed to be introspective. Suddenly, with a heartbreaking look on her face, she said she had to leave. She had eaten her dinner and wanted to leave. She hugged April, and that show of affection shocked her good friend. They were close, but Chantal was never given to outward affection for anyone. April was suddenly worried and asked if she should accompany her home. Chantal assured her she was fine, that she wanted to be alone. So they said their goodbyes and each went separate ways.

April had a strange feeling as she thought about the evening's turn of events. She still couldn't believe Chantal's tale of a Hollywood life and an actress for a mother. April called Shane with the news that Chantal was indeed Tina. Shane promptly called Emily with the news. Emily was excited but reminded herself that the information was not hers to pass along. Chantal would ultimately make the decision to contact her mother if that's what in her heart she wanted to do.

Chantal had not been able to shut her mind off to go to sleep. Memories of her childhood, her mom, and the men that had come to her bedroom floated through her mind. She awoke, wondering if last evening's episode had actually happened. *Yes,* she concluded as she stepped into the shower, *it had indeed occurred.* She had told April about her former life and shared a part of herself that she had buried and thought forever gone, forever forgotten. Chantal looked at the paper she had pulled out of her pocket with the name and number of the discoverer. "Emily," she said. A person named Emily had dragged memories of her unhappy, scary years growing up into the light of day. As she prepared to go to work, she asked herself if she was ready to face those days, to let them surface.

The courthouse was busy as usual, and she was preoccupied. She struggled to keep her mind on cases and found herself being just a bit more lenient than usual. A raised eyebrow from one of the prosecutors brought her back to her old self, and she again showed no mercy to criminals standing before her.

As the day ended, she felt particularly exhausted. The little sleep she had managed the night before had been fitful and full of frightening dreams. Hopefully, she could relax this evening and get a good night's rest. Chantal hadn't given much thought to being alone in life until now, but she suddenly *felt* alone. She had lived this way for years, preferring it to having a roommate or a husband. Why did it make a difference now? She was still the same person, although she didn't quite consider herself to be the same; but she couldn't put her finger on why. Was she so different just because she told her friend April about her old life? Had everything really changed just because she had divulged her past? She wasn't wanted by the police. Well, at least not for the secret she had just revealed.

She studied the phone number. Should she call? Could she bring herself to touch those numbers on her phone? What would she say, and what did she actually want to know about her mother? For the first time in years, much to her surprise, tears came to her eyes. Crying had never been a product of her emotions. She had toughened up at a young age and did not let her guard down—until now, when she was overcome with sobs.

When the waterworks ended, she felt calm. Without giving it another thought, she dialed the number and soon heard a female voice answering with a friendly "Hello."

"Hello, Emily, this is Chantal McAllister, well...actually...Tina Fitzgerald," Chantal said and quickly added. "I was given your number by my friend April."

Emily was now aware of who this was and quite surprised. There was an uneasy silence at first, as neither knew exactly how to begin the conversation.

"I'm the one who is redecorating your mother's home," said Emily to start the conversation. "Your mother believes you are dead." Hearing only silence, Emily chastised herself for speaking so bluntly.

"I wondered why she didn't even look for me," replied a subdued Chantal.

"She did," Emily quickly answered, defending Sybil. Emily went on to tell her about the police not taking her disappearance seriously and reminded her of her rebellious days, leading the police to believe she left of her own free will, which of course she had. Emily was on a roll, defending Sybil. She told Chantal of her mother's fear for her daughter's safety and her acceptance that her Tina was gone forever. Emily also told about her mother's gigolo who was quite possibly taking her for everything he could before running off with another unsuspecting older woman.

"I don't know what to do." Chantal's attitude was feeling kindly toward her mother one minute and angry with her the next for her lousy parenting.

"Think about it, and we'll talk again in a couple days," Emily said, stating what seemed to be a logical idea. Chantal needed time to process all the information, and Emily needed time to think of suggestions for a solution.

Emily was an optimist and wanted everything to work out. She wanted Sybil and Tina to reunite, to forgive, and to be in each other's lives again. Emily's own mother, who had died young, had greatly influenced her belief that families needed to find a way to be together. She had her own family problems and was determined to do her best to work things out with her father and her brother.

CHAPTER 27

"Feelin' Good"

———◆———

EMILY'S RETURN TO HIDDEN RAPIDS was a good reason for another party at Stonebridge. Shane drove up from Minneapolis, and Stone and Billie had a fire roaring on the beach when she drove in. Emily had not been away long, but it felt like a lengthy time to her. There was something about this North Country that drew her back. She was aware of a compelling attraction to the area. Was it the locale or more an emotional pull calling her back? She didn't know.

Guests at the resort and friends from the area joined in the party on the smooth sandy beach. Hot dogs, chips, salads, and later S'mores added to the delightful evening. Emily had many emotions running through her as she settled into the little cabin that had recently been traded to the resort for a newer larger chalet at the end of the complex. She would continue staying in the cabin until she had time to put the finishing touches on her family's new place.

Emily had already searched through interior decorating magazines for ideas on turning the old buildings at Stonebridge into more modern looking vacation hide-aways. A comfortable, casual style would enhance the weary look of the cabins. The interiors would need to be ready to withstand wet swimsuits and crowds of guests with barbeque-slathered plates. Nothing in the cabin would be luxurious or too pretty. Furniture would be sturdy and capable of handling rambunctious youngsters and partying adults. Bedspreads would have a soft comfortable appeal. She would rummage around the storage room to see if something old could be refurbished and used once again. Sometimes the old in redecorating becomes the new and latest trend.

She greeted Kirsten with a warm hello and smile as she entered the lodge. The two had become friends as had Shane and Stone. The four had spent many hours together on the beach, and Kirsten had roamed the antique shops with Emily on her days off. Stone was sitting in the lobby with Kirsten drinking coffee. They had become quite an item, and Emily could see the love in Stone's eyes whenever he looked at her or even spoke her name.

Fall had arrived and the leaves were beginning to turn. Bedroom windows were being closed more often, and there were fewer days for sandals and shorts. Geese flew overhead, honking as they migrated south. A green algae bloom lay heavily on the surface of many lakes. Docks and boatlifts were being pulled out of the water, signaling the end of the summer season.

Billie had been given every test imaginable with still no concrete diagnoses for what continued to ail her. Her doctor had called in a specialist in cardiology. He knew there was certainly something. She had endured countless blood draws, a colonoscopy, an endoscopy, a CT scan, and an MRI, as well as stress tests and ultrasounds. Yet there seemed to be no answer for what was wrong.

Roxanne's house was coming along nicely—ready for the final touches. Emily also continued working on redecorating the cabins. The structure remodeling had been completed and they all sported new windows, roofs, shingles, and doors.

Roxanne's new home looked magnificent, embraced by its surroundings, with lakeshore curving around the site on three sides. The prized peninsula setting had proved an exciting challenge for the designer. Roxanne had wanted to accommodate large gatherings with panoramic water views from as many rooms as possible. The need for a large house may have been only a dream, but Roxanne had visions of family gatherings—summer partiers spilling out onto the deck or holiday gatherings when there was snow outside. She longed for a home that made people feel comfortable and happy.

Emily, Holly, and Roxanne had spent many hours roaming the stores in Duluth and also Hidden Rapids. Roxanne had urged Holly to do the decision-making and shopping for her. However, they wanted *her* to be a part of picking things out. With Roxanne's permission Emily had consulted with Roxanne's therapist several times, who wanted Roxanne to choose as many of her own things as possible. The therapist stressed that Roxanne needed to be a part of choosing her personal items and articles for her home, such as dishes, pot and pans, silverware, and appliances. Making those decisions would give her confidence and also the feeling that they were hers. The compulsion to gather possessions around her had to be overcome, but what she chose would feel essential to her day-to-day living.

Emily took great pains in helping Roxanne select accessories without adding clutter. She wanted Roxanne's home to look clean and inviting, emphasizing great fabrics, texture, and fresh colors. "Less is more," Emily said often, repeating it as Roxanne reached for more *stuff* while they shopped. Roxanne's home with its open floor plan incorporating kitchen, dining room, and great room gave a sense of spaciousness. The soft curves of rolled-arm sofas and sculptured armchairs extended an invitation to kick back. At the end of the room, a massive rock fireplace soothed the spirit. Hanging above the focal point of the space was a picture of Roxanne's children and grandchildren combined by a local frame shop into one magnificent photo collage.

Decorating the upstairs bedrooms where guests (hopefully grandchildren) would stay was kept serene through simple wicker furnishings and calming yet compelling colors. Emily picked a large range of blues, gray, and sea green, adding accents of purple and lime green to stand out against the dark blue of Lake Pokegama. The master bedroom boasted creamy neutrals and soothing black and white photography. During the summer, the French doors would be flung open to foster a seamless indoor-outdoor connection. Off the upstairs bedrooms was a picturesque balcony where visitors could soak up the sun. White wainscoting and pale blue walls adorned the bathroom that sat between the two bedrooms.

Roxanne was particularly nervous when Emily picked her up for their trip to Duluth for more shopping because Holly had invited Roxanne and Jack for dinner. Roxanne had almost made herself ill just thinking about the invitation. Her anxiety was evident when she got into the car. Emily tried to talk about the house and the decisions that still needed to be made, but Roxanne remained focused on the dinner party that night. Emily turned the car around and headed back to Stonebridge. There was no need to make decorating decisions that very day, and Emily needed Billie's help to settle Roxanne down.

Coffee and cookies at Stonebridge were a fine interruption for Roxanne. Emily gently brought up dinner plans and conveyed her worry about Roxanne's stress. Billie put her arms around her dear friend and hugged her hard. Roxanne burst into tears, and they all had a good cry.

"It's what I have been praying for, and now that I am asked to come—to have a meal at my daughter's—I am scared to death. I feel like I could be ill. My stomach is churning, and I actually think I could faint."

Emily and Billie reminded Roxanne what she had been taught to do when she felt anxious or frightened; and it worked. The calming sessions she had practiced with her therapist brought her back to feeling somewhat normal, though still a bit apprehensive, about the evening. She called Jack, and he was excited to pick her up. Emily and Billie helped her decide what she should wear. They were now almost as nervous about the dinner party as Roxanne. She went home to get ready for the night as Emily and Billie encouraged her to enjoy a good visit with her family.

When Jack knocked on the door above the boathouse, Roxanne opened it looking fabulous. She was wearing the perfect outfit—a white skirt, purple blouse, and white chunky sandals.

"You look great!" he exclaimed, squeezing her hand.

"I'm so scared," she said, a tear slipping down her check.

"I'm right here with you all the way. Just stay by me and you'll be fine. Holly loves you. Just remember that."

Roxanne wished the drive to Holly's had been farther. She needed more time to reign in her fear. She didn't know if she could trust herself to act the way she was supposed to, that is, *expected* to. It had been so long since she had been around strangers for any length of time, and these people were in essence strangers. While lately she had seen Holly for lunch on a regular basis, that had felt like a controlled environment. She hadn't seen her grandchildren in such a long time. Would they even know her? Would they want to? Those questions haunted her.

As Jack maneuvered the car down the driveway, Holly's Siberian Husky raced toward them. His name was Freeway, and he was friendly. Roxanne remembered their getting him as a puppy, so he was getting old now. He welcomed them with a wagging tail and friendly licks. Jack rang the doorbell, and a pleasant-faced youngster invited them to come in. Another youngster reached around and grabbed Roxanne in a hug and cried excitedly, "Grandma!" Five-year-old Abby hugged her around her knees. Connor, age 8, and Abby, age 5, were exuberant at the sight of their grandmother. Eric, age 12, named after his uncle, was more reserved; but he, too, was smiling. Holly had a hug for each, and Josh had a hug for Roxanne and a firm handshake for Jack.

Dinner was simple, delicious, comfort food: roast beef, mashed potatoes, gravy, and a hearty salad. Topping off the evening was coffee and strawberry ice cream. Their evening ended with hugs and tears and the promise of another meal together soon. A sigh of relief and sitting close to Jack in the car, like they used to years ago when they were teenagers and dating, brought the night to a perfect ending.

CHAPTER 28

"CALIFORNIA DREAMING"

———◆———

A MESSY SLOW-MOVING EARLY WINTER storm churned out of Canada into the northern United States, bringing with it ice, sleet, and heavy, wet snow. Slippery roads were creating havoc along the northern tier of North Dakota, Minnesota, and Wisconsin. Drivers fought poor visibility as warnings were issued to stay off the roads. The coldest weather of the winter season came barreling into the North Country accompanied by dangerously high winds. Homeowners were being warned about how the added weight on rooftops could cause them to collapse. The biting cold and early snowstorm was blamed for many heart attacks across the three states. As the snow accumulated on the ground, roads froze, cars ran out of gas, and tractor-trailers jackknifed. Highways turned into parking lots. The storm paralyzed the entire Upper Midwest.

Multicar pile-ups caused by whiteouts had emergency room doctors and nurses working overtime. Some of the medical staff stayed at the hospital, as traveling to their homes was not possible. Schools and business were closed, and the bitter cold prompted many to crank up their furnaces and wood stoves.

Many were unprepared. Chimneys had not been cleaned, so calls to the fire department had exhausted the volunteers, and several homes were destroyed. Helicopters took to the sky to search for stranded drivers. Snowmobiles were used to deliver food, water, and gas or rides home to people stuck on the roads. The winter storm had walloped the north.

Students were trapped on buses over night, huddling to keep warm. Many stayed in schools where backup generators stayed busy.

Stone checked on Emily several times a day. She often invited him in for a cup of coffee and assured him that she had prepared for the storm. Emily hadn't been in one for 20 years and had actually been a bit excited about the prospect. A large stack of split wood sat just outside her door, and she had stocked up on food that did not have to be heated. She hoped the electricity would not be off but was ready for that, too. Her biggest problem was not being able to be charge her cell phone, but people once lived without cell phones, too, she reminded herself.

Before the fiercest part of the storm had even arrived, Emily was having trouble keeping her cabin even almost comfortable with her wood burning fireplace and a space heater that scared the daylights out of her. She didn't dare to use it during the night, fearing it would start a fire. She slept on an old couch close to the stove and awoke each morning with a painful backache.

After her morning coffee and toast, she braved the snow and cold and continued decorating the cabins despite the frigid temperatures. A braided rug set the cabin tone in each of the buildings. Long farm tables gave guests ample space to eat inside if necessary. Emily made sure each room had shelves and plenty of pegs for hanging clothes, towels, or swimwear. The kitchens were equipped with everything needed for cooking delicious meals, and grills sat on every deck. She had chosen a rich looking black, wheat, and tan quilt for one cabin, a green plaid print for another. A muted blue, red, and tan caught her eye for the cabin called Sunny Skies. She made sure there was good lighting and plenty of small end tables where books could be set aside while catching up on resort activities. Cabins needed eye-pleasing pieces but functional to be a comfortable retreat. She genuinely believed Frank Lloyd Wright's rule, "Form follows function."

Shane called her often and occasionally would come to Hidden Rapids for the weekend. Their relationship had turned into comfortable love.

The vicious winter weather was keeping many in during the harsh cold months. Emily visited her father as often as she could although she knew, but hated to admit, that Lucy did a good job of taking care of Paul. Emily had planned to return to California before spring and by that time had hoped to decide where she would call home. A call from Chantal McAllister speeded her trip up a little. Chantal had asked if there was someone who could be with her mother should she decide to fly out to see her. She was worried that the news might cause her to experience a panic attack or worse a heart attack.

"She has her personal assistant," Emily assured her. Rita had been with Sybil for many years even before Chantal left.

"Could you be there, too?" Chantal asked, as if it were no big deal for Emily to fly back to LA. "I'd like to be there—see her in person—but not upset her too much. That's why I think it would help if you were there, too."

Emily struggled with the decision of going to Hollywood with Chantal. She was ecstatic that there may be a reunion in the works but didn't feel as if she needed to be a part of it. She had already learned, even with her few and short conversations with Chantal, that there was nothing shy or unassuming about her.

Emily talked it over with Shane. He didn't try to influence her but did remind her that a meeting between the estranged mother and daughter would obviously be awkward. He added that perhaps the addition of Rita and Emily would temper the drama.

The thought of a few warm days away from cold Minnesota would be enjoyable, and Emily did have a few loose ends to take care of in California. She had decided to give up her apartment there and put her furniture in storage, intending to return there sometime so why not now.

Chantal had been on the phone with Rita, who was skeptical of the long-time-missing daughter's intentions. She had been Sybil's friend and employee for many years and was adamant that Chantal not cause Sybil any more heartache. With that assurance, Rita agreed be a part of planning this reunion. She and Emily would prepare Sybil for the return of her prodigal daughter.

Emily and Chantal boarded the same plane, sat next to each other, but hardly spoke a word to one another. The once uncontrollable young woman was quiet and calm. Thoughts of long ago filled her mind, and she struggled with the memories of childhood. The past loomed large in her mind, and the struggle between anger and forgiveness battled inside of her.

After landing, they rented cars. Emily went to her condo, and Chantal drove to her hotel. They would meet the next morning on the road in front of the lane to Sybil's home.

Emily called to make arrangements with a storage company, and they would send a truck and two workers to load up her things the next afternoon.

Chantal walked the floor in her lovely hotel room, her mind filled with pictures of long ago. Her mother's smile sometimes floated gently through her thoughts, and she could almost smell the Shalimar her mother once wore. She normally had great control and didn't like the fear that was coursing through her body. There was no way to predict how this reunion would go—no way to know if her mother would be happy to see her, or furious for all Chantal had put her through. A warm shower and a straight brandy sent her quickly asleep.

Emily was on the phone to Rita and Chantal the next morning. Emily would arrive first and set the stage with Rita to ease Sybil into the news of Chantal's return. Emily didn't know what they should call her: Tina or Chantal.

Rita met her at the door. They spoke briefly before Sybil invited her into the breakfast nook. Gooey cinnamon rolls and hot coffee greeted her. Rita joined them also. She had been a part of Sybil's family for years but rarely joined her when guests were there. Sybil gave her a questioning look but moved on to say how much she loved the way Emily's choices of décor had made her home come alive to reflect Sybil's tastes of former Hollywood days yet with a contemporary flare.

Emily began their mission by telling the story of watching four friends enjoying a dinner out and the envy she had felt, watching the four professionals together. She told of the fun they were having and the particular beauty of one of the women.

"She looked like Tina," Rita said, staring into Sybil's eyes. As she reached over and took Sybil's hand, she choked back a sob.

"What's wrong?" Sybil questioned, as she looked at both of the women.

"Your Tina is here. She's waiting outside the door, hoping you'll welcome her in," Rita said pleadingly. Sybil held her breath in shock and disbelief.

Emily went to the door. Opening it, she saw Tina—pale and frightened. The next moment was chaotic. Sybil rushed past Emily and reached for her daughter. They hugged and cried for several minutes.

Emily and Rita smiled and congratulated themselves on the morning's reunion and drank more coffee. Sybil and Chantal went outside and sat by the pool, their feet dangling in the warm water. They would each need time, understanding, and forgiveness to mend the hurt and anguish they had caused each other.

Emily left after a tasty noon lunch. Rex was there, too. He had walked out to the pool as the mother and daughter reunion was taking place.

Emily had storage business to deal with that afternoon, and a few other errands to run. The next morning she called Chantal to tell her she would be flying back to Minnesota that evening. Chantal said the visit with her mother was going remarkably well, and she hoped Sybil would be visiting her in Duluth soon.

"Oh, by the way," Chantal said, sounding smug. "Rex is leaving. We had a talk. I made him an offer he couldn't refuse."

CHAPTER 29

"I CAN SEE CLEARLY NOW"

———◆———

EMILY HAD ALMOST FINISHED DECORATING the cabins but wanted to check out the *treasures* that might be hiding in the upstairs storage room. The door squeaked as Emily turned the knob and pushed it open. A chill came over her, and her breath quickened. An ache in her chest suddenly flowed through her and a throbbing in her brain made her fear her head would explode. It seemed as if someone—something—was forcing her to the back of the room, to the windows overlooking the rear of the resort. The images that appeared below and the voices she heard caused her to convulse. The trembling invaded her entire body and she fell to the floor. A bitterly cold wind blew through the room, and Jenny's ghost sat perched on the high box by the window. Emily left the room, running as fast as she could down the stairs and past a surprised Stone and Kirsten.

Emily frantically jumped into her Lexus and roared down the gravel road. Thoughts were whirling in her mind, and she felt as if she were spiraling out of control. Any control she once had left her the instant she dared to remember what she had seen. She had been looking out the window and saw her very best friend in a pink corduroy jumper with a frilly white blouse underneath. She had leaned against the window as Josh pushed his way close beside her for a better look out the attic window. There had been a full moon and the two could see several people standing beneath the heavy pines.

Jenny, Emily, and Josh had come running out of the dining area in the lodge and were headed for the upstairs to listen to music when Jenny's father had yelled up the stairs for Jenny. He had said there was to be a prayer meeting behind the lodge, and the Ruler had said to be sure to bring Jenny.

"Hide and watch, watch from the attic window above the swing," Jenny had said in a disturbing tone, a pitch Emily had never heard before. "And tell—watch and tell," Jenny had said. "You must tell everything you see—no matter who and what you see." She had sounded composed yet terrified.

A man had held Jenny from behind as another had slashed her neck. Bright red blood flowed from her throat. Moonlight shined on the blood that dripped onto the pine needles and dirt. Jenny's long auburn hair fell over her face as she rolled on her side, jerked, and then stopped moving.

Shock had held them in suspension for a few seconds before they ran into another bedroom. They couldn't speak. Josh had sobbed. Emily had gasped for air and huddled in a corner of the room. Josh was quickly in the corner too.

"What's happening?" Emily sobbed. "What did we see?"

Emily and Josh had hugged each other, their hearts pounding.

"We have to tell. Jenny said to tell what we saw—whatever we saw," Josh had whispered. Emily had left him and ran out of the room. Josh followed her, running down the stairs, almost clipping her heels. They ran to their family's cabin, still crying. Their parents had gone out for dinner and they were alone. Emily had run into her room and Josh into his. Sleep came fitfully.

Neither Emily nor Josh had recalled any of it the next day. Their minds had protected them from the shock, blocking absolutely any recollection of the violent sight they had witnessed. Their brains must have sought to shelter them from the cruel act each had witnessed, storing it away where it could not hurt them. When Billie had returned from shopping and she had wondered where Jenny was, Jenny's father had said she had gone swimming. Jenny often had a swim before bedtime, so Billie had not felt alarmed.

Josh's driveway came into view, and Emily drove like a crazy person down his lane. Gravel hit the sides of the car as she left a cloud of dust behind her vehicle. She knocked frantically and hoped Josh would not be the one to answer. If Holly came to the door, she would at least let Emily in. Her wish was not to be. Instead, it was Josh, who looked at his sister with contempt and hostility.

"What do you want?" he snarled. His words were not welcoming, but he did not appear to be intoxicated. She had feared he would be drunk, unable to carry on a conversation with her and simply throw her out.

"I asked you what you wanted! Why are you here standing at my door?" Josh shouted.

Holly came running into the living room. "Emily!" she said with a shocked look on her face. She reached out to hug her.

Josh interrupted the reunion with a growl. "You're not welcome. We don't want you here." With each word his voice became louder until he was screaming at Emily, spitting the words "get out" in her face. Towering over her, he hadn't actually touched her, but she felt the heat of his breath.

Emily had stood mute, but now she was angry—angry about losing her brother and her close friend. She felt furious because he wouldn't talk about what was stuck in his craw. She stood firm as he stared her down while screaming at her. She screamed back. The memory she had just recalled was ghastly, beyond horrific. Was it true? She had to know.

"Do you...remember a murder?" she shrieked.

"Yeah, I remember. So what!"

"Do you remember Jenny's murder?"

"Yes, I remember, and we didn't tell. We were too scared. We were cowards." His voice was calm, alarmingly calm.

"The memory just flashed back to me less than half an hour ago. I remembered nothing until today. I walked into the storeroom at Stonebridge and it came to me."

Josh circled the room, prowling like a lion. Holly stood in disbelief. Jenny's murder? She couldn't wrap her mind around what was going on in her living room.

"Sit down, Josh," she said sternly. "Emily, come sit over here by me." Holly patted the cushion on the couch next to her. "We're going to have a calm discussion about what you have been saying."

Emily and Josh each listened to the other's picture of that awful day. Josh's recall had come first in brief dreams and flashes of sights and sounds. He had believed that Emily knew all along and hated that she wasn't telling the authorities. His mind would fluctuate: sometimes he believed the murder had actually happened; sometimes he thought he was just having nightmares.

Alcohol had soothed his nerves and numbed his conscience, and the nightmares had come less often. He would go on a real bender after having the recurrent dream of Jenny's throat being slit. Fire would flare in his nightmare, and often he would feel burned. He hated even to see Emily because the sight of her would make the scene below the window at Stonebridge appeared more vivid. Jenny's final plea haunted him. The faces were a blur in his dreams. Only Jenny's was perfectly clear, her bright red blood, pooled on the ground.

"We need to go back to Stonebridge, to the storage room. Together, our subconscious minds may remember. Maybe standing there together again will help us see a real picture of what happened that night." Emily put her arm around her brother. He reluctantly walked with her to her car.

The drive to Stonebridge was quiet. Emily didn't mind telling Josh that she was scared, that she was afraid to walk into that room again, and terrified to remember. Who would the people be who were standing there watching the Ruler? Would they know the murderer? Emily knew there had been many followers of the cult leader at the fire. The church where the services normally were held was atop a hill and somewhat secluded. But for some reason that night, that particular night, the members had gathered behind the resort.

The gossip in town had ranged from satanic worship to sex abuse. Many women had supposedly been encouraged to leave their husbands if they didn't want to embrace the religion. Distrust of the Ruler and authorities looking into the cult's dealings with the local businesses had eventually forced the Devils out of town.

Billie's husband had been caught up in the religious sect. Billie would have no part of it and was unhappy with his participation. Jenny loved her father and had gone with him mostly because he didn't want to go alone. She frowned on the behavior of many in the cult and tried desperately to talk her dad out of going to that church. Jim was searching for something, and obviously that particular sect spoke to him.

Stone was still in the lodge at the resort with Kirsten when Emily and Josh arrived. Billie had gone into the hospital that morning for more tests. Emily told Stone they needed to go up to the storeroom. Stone was bewildered but didn't ask any questions. He knew about the longtime rift between Emily and Josh and was surprised to see Josh standing beside her.

With Stone's okay they made their way up the stairs to the door of the storeroom. Hesitating for a few seconds, Josh turned the knob and they were in. It was full of totes and boxes, Christmas trees, decorations, extra bedding, and quilts. A small pathway led to the far end of the room where large windows overlooked the back yard of the lodge. Emily closed her eyes for a minute and then dared to look down. The huge old fire pit still stood just below the window. Years ago it had been only a small cleared area with large pines hiding some of the cabins. Now it was a wide-open area with full view of the older log cabins.

"I'm trying hard to think," she told Josh with a nervous laugh. She could imagine the fire and the bright moon shining down on the people. There had been a crowd. Josh and Emily hadn't been the only ones to witness the terror of that night.

"I see many," Josh spoke slowly. "I can see a man holding Jenny down, but I don't see a face. I can see the knife and the blood, but again, I don't see a face."

"I see a woman in the crowd." Emily's voice was suddenly hushed. "I see Lucy—a young Lucy standing in the background almost behind the trees with the light from the fire flicking in her face."

"Are you sure it's Lucy?" Josh shook his head wondering if Emily could be right. "I mean, I know you don't like her. I don't either, but I don't see her there—not yet anyway."

Emily thought back on Lucy's statement about stirring things up. Maybe she worried about Emily's memory of this murder. But how would she know? No one knew what Emily and Josh had seen. Just then in Emily's mind's eye, she saw a worker come out. He had lit a fire in the pit, and a few cult members had begun to gather. She recalled seeing a fire dart around the kindling that had been used to start it. The fire had crept in between the dry logs that had been placed over the smaller sticks.

Josh began to weep uncontrollably, nodded his head and said, "I see her. I do see Lucy. She's wearing a white blouse and a red sweater. Oh, my God! That mortician…Old Man Bennett…he's the one holding Jenny." Emily and Josh spoke in unison as their brains clicked, at long last turning their memories on. Recall scrolled through their minds like a movie in slow motion. The Ruler had slit Jenny's throat and her father had wailed out a loud scream that would have been heard for miles around. Emily had covered her ears as the screams burst into her head. Josh, daring to remember, had heard them, too. Jenny's father had certainly not been aware of what was about to happen. Two college students who had returned for a homecoming game, Brian and Elliot, were leaning on a pine tree, casually watching the gore.

Okay, they were done in *that* room and made their way quickly downstairs. Stone asked what was wrong, because the looks on Emily and Josh's faces were disturbing.

"Nothing, we're fine; we just have to get going right away. We'll talk later," Emily said as they walked out the door.

Deciding they would drive immediately to the sheriff's office, they sped toward town. Each had much information in their heads they wanted to unload as quickly as possible. They walked into the sheriff's office together with red eyes from a torrent of tears and clear thoughts about the sight they had seen so many years ago.

Describing the horrendous memory sent beads of sweat and rushes of tears. Suddenly they felt like they were teens again, recalling a surreal tale of murder and conspiracy. Sobbing echoed around the room and filtered into the adjoining offices. A deputy peeked his head into the office, wondering if help was needed.

When they left the sheriff's office, Josh brought Emily back to the resort. Their faces were pale and drawn as they walked into the lodge. Stone and Kirsten could hardly believe the story they told.

Stone had news for them, too. Billie had been in the hospital for more tests when she had a seizure and almost died. She was having emergency brain surgery as they spoke. Kirsten would stay in the office overnight, and Roxanne was coming in the morning to help run the business. Stone was going to spend the night at the hospital. The doctor had wanted to transfer her to the Duluth hospital or Abbott Northwestern in Minneapolis, but Billie was out of time. Josh would stay the night with Emily in the old cabin. They had so much to talk about and years to sort through.

Sheriff Emerson didn't waste any time driving to Northern Exposure and knocking on Lucy's door. She was in Paul's apartment and heard the sheriff call her name. "I have some questions for you, Lucy. We should talk in private." Emerson was all business, and Lucy had a sinking feeling that trouble had come calling. They sat in the living room of her apartment as he described Emily and Josh's rendition of the night at Stonebridge Resort a lifetime ago. Color drained from Lucy's face and she sobbed, admitting at long last that she had indeed witnessed the sacrifice of the young woman the cult called the Lamb: Jenny. She told the sheriff that the Ruler and the mortician had carried the young sacrifice away and that she had later heard that the authorities believed Jenny had drowned.

The sheriff didn't know what would happen next—if anything. The children there were just that—children. None were adults at the time and so much time had passed. The killer was dead and even the other adults who had been present were either dead or elderly, and many no longer lived in the area.

Emerson left, leaving Lucy to worry and cry. He didn't tell Paul anything, although Paul had opened his door so he could come in, had he chosen to do so. Lucy would have a lot of explaining to do. Emerson slowly got into his car. He had a real mess to deal with—many questions and, at least for the moment, no answers.

Emerson's phone rang before he had returned to the office. It was the manager at Northern Exposure. Lucy had suffered what appeared to have been a heart attack almost the minute he left; Paul had walked into her apartment just as she collapsed.

Stone spent the night with Billie, and Roxanne came to Stonebridge in the morning. When Stone returned to the resort, Roxanne took his place at the hospital. Billie was in ICU, her frail body stuck with IVs, needles, and monitors of all sorts. Roxanne gently stroked her dear friend's arm and wiped away a succession of salty tears that were running down her face. She hadn't come this far in renewing their friendship to lose her now.

Roxanne prayed for Billie, calling on God to let her live. Hours in the hospital turned into days. She wiped Billie's forehead with cool washcloths and talked of the old days—of the three musketeers: Charlotte, Billie, and Roxanne. The doctors were gravely concerned that Billie was not responding and waking as quickly from the surgery as had been expected. They did not consider her to be comatose but rather drifting in and out of deep sleep.

Roxanne sat with Billie and talked to her steadily. She reminisced about their young days, their swim team, and old loves. She brought music from their era. Rock 'n' Roll filled the room with Elvis singing "Hound Dog" and that sexy-voiced Ricky Nelson singing "Lonesome Town." Finally Billy awoke. Roxanne squealed in excitement for the nurse, and soon the room was filled with medical personnel. It was a joyous day. Billie was on her way to recovery.

CHAPTER 30

"I HEARD IT THROUGH THE GRAPEVINE"

Roxanne's house was finished and she was excited, pleased with her new home. Barry had stopped over to talk about the spec house to be built on another part of the property. He would need an easement to bring the electrical and telephone lines to the lakeshore she had sold to him. She was happy to sign the waiver.

They sat on the deck listening to the loons cry and watching the ducks move smoothly through the just melted water. Spring had arrived in the North Country. It was a new beginning for Roxanne as well. She had arranged to have a personal organizer visit her once a week for a while. If the woman saw that Roxanne was doing well, she would taper her visits off to once every two weeks. It would be a gradual process.

Her therapist would still see her every week for the time being. Emily had finished the last minute decorating touches but stopped by to check in on Roxanne often. Billie needed Roxanne at the resort, and Roxanne had attended church a few times with Jack. Life felt almost normal—that is, if she actually remembered what normal was.

The trenching machines, digging a trough for electricity and telephone, moved slowly along the far edge of the Abbott family cemetery, which overlooked the lake. Three men walked alongside the trencher, making sure the operator had a clear path for the equipment. A loud, horrified voice prompted the man running the apparatus to come to an abrupt stop. One of the men picked up a long bone and, looking puzzled, gave it a kick, knocking off the dirt that clung to it. As he moved to pick it up, his boot loosened a mound of dirt and a skull rolled forward.

Astonishment showed on the faces of the four men. The man running the trencher stopped the machine and examined the find. He thought for a short time about the fact that they were in a cemetery. Bones might be found, but, after thinking it over, he dialed 9-1-1. His words came out fast. "We've found bones—a skull and what looks like a leg bone. Send a deputy to Abbott cemetery."

"Don't touch anything," he said to the men standing by the skull, which was void of anything except teeth. They had backed up a little, sickened by their discovery.

The noise of tires on gravel broke the silence as the squad car drove up and parked alongside the trencher. He put gloves on and reached in to retrieve a bag from the back seat of the car.

"What have we got here?" the deputy asked as he reached for the long bone lying next to the skull. He slipped it into the bag and then picked up the skull. "Could it be one of the Abbott relatives?" he asked, loud enough so the group of men heard him even though he was mostly talking to himself.

"No," the machine handler spoke up. "We have a diagram of the graves buried here, and we were digging far away from the nearest burial site. But maybe a dog could have dug up one of the graves. Some of them are really old and probably didn't have much for a coffin."

The deputy listened and then called in the discovery. The noise of more squad cars broke the serene ambiance of the lake. Roxanne and Jack followed the patrol cars down the pathway by the cemetery. It was barely wide enough for a car to get through. Car doors banged shut, shattering the silence. The racket annoyed Roxanne, and Jack demanded to know what was going on.

"We've found a skull and a femur here and need to investigate further." Sheriff Emerson had arrived and attempted to calm Roxanne and Jack.

"You're standing right next to a cemetery—an old cemetery. Some animal might have dug a bone up. We have bears around, too, you know." Jack was irritated mostly because Roxanne was so disturbed. She hadn't been to this part of her property for years, and finding herself here with no warning and chance to prepare for the trauma was extremely disturbing.

Jack coaxed her into leaving the area and drove her home. He sat with her and wrapped his arms tightly around her. Thank goodness tomorrow was her scheduled appointment with her therapist. Roxanne had an anxiety pill to take when—if—things got hairy. She needed it now, and Jack was quick to get her medication and a glass of water. He stayed with her until she slept.

After Jack and Roxanne had left the area, an agent from the Minnesota Bureau of Criminal Apprehension arrived. Their man in Hidden Rapids was at the site in less than an hour. Kirsten would have been the first called, but she was continuing her undercover work at Stonebridge. She had received a call about the discovery, but her job at the resort was not finished. BCA also called Shane, a proficient coroner and their expert forensics investigator. He would be there the next morning.

In the meantime, the local coroner, Elliot Bennett, was called for advice on how to protect the site from animals that might roam the area at night. The animals would likely drag bones away from the site if possible. Elliot got the call on his cell phone. He was in Deer River picking up a body. He finished loading the corpse and called Brian to ask, "What the hell's going on?"

"What are you talking about?"

"I just got a call from the sheriff to come to the Abbott Cemetery. Bodies are coming up around the trenching machines."

"What trenching machines?"

Cheryl saw the look of terror on Brian's face. Her stomach churned; she knew danger had arrived.

CHAPTER 31

"A Careless Whisper"

BRITTANY BENNETT WOULD NOT PERMIT the scandal that was rocking the community to impede her usual spring party. She would host a gathering to celebrate Ice Out for the neighbors on Lake Pokegama. Although some lake residents were not as wealthy as Brittany and Elliot, she wanted to appear to be just an ordinary person to them—if only just once a year.

Brittany wanted their get-away on Pokegama Lake to be called a beach house or cottage. The word *cabin* meant logs and rustic living, and *rustic* in any way, shape, or form was not for her. She believed their cottage should capitalize on its gorgeous surroundings as much as possible, and her decorator had made sure their *get-away* lived up to that expectation.

Brittany loved to host the elite of Hidden Rapids. An open floor plan made entertaining easy. A large L-shaped room incorporated the kitchen with its white cabinets, granite countertops, and a white marble tile backsplash. A dining area and family room with teal cushions contrasted nicely with the dark rattan chairs in the family room. It gave the place a stylish look and coordinated with the natural colors of the surrounding scenery.

She and Elliot would host a party for a few fortunate Pokegama Lake residents on Saturday night. She would invite Billie and Stone of course. Their resort was not far from Brittany's cottage, and Elliot occasionally had to use their boat ramp to launch their craft early in the season.

Roxanne and Jack would be invited also. Brittany had heard that Roxanne was feeling better and that she had moved into her new home. Elliot liked to cultivate good relationships with business owners and also the lake residents. His funeral business was lucrative, and he had worked hard to keep it that way.

Townspeople knew Brittany thought herself upper class, that they should consider it a privilege if she deigned to speak to them. Elliot on the other hand was friendly and caring. He needed to portray himself as humble and compassionate. He actually *was* more caring than Brittany, even though certain aspects of his life haunted him.

The sun was just setting as the party began. The weather was mild with just a slight breeze off the lake. A fire danced in the fire pit, and guests sat around the flames, enjoying evening cocktails. Roxanne and Jack arrived, followed closely by Stone and Kirsten. Shane had been visiting Emily and was also included in the invitation.

The napkins were bright orange and the plates a soft, marine blue. Reflections of the sunset and the water heightened the inviting look of the table. Seashells were used as place markers. Air plants were tucked into a variety of shells, large and small. Twinkling candles in various sizes of translucent votives kept the table fun and casual. Brittany's caterer had taken care of everything, assuring her that this would be a night to remember.

The main course was Italian Seafood Stew served with a bountiful green salad, French bread with Rosemary-Garlic Dipping Oil, and topped off with Limoncello Sorbet. The guests felt like royalty. It certainly was a night and meal fit for a king.

Emily loved the fact that Roxanne had been brave enough to come. Jack was by her side every minute, but it took courage to be in the public eye here with some people she knew but also with a few strangers.

After the meal, the guests again adjourned to the chairs by the fire and were served an after dinner drink. Emily needed to use the restroom and was ushered into the magnificent beach house by one of the servers. As she walked by the living room, she saw her host talking in hushed tones to Brian. As she walked by them, having to get a bit close to navigate the hallway to the bathroom, Brian whispered something in Elliot's ear. Emily's stomach churned and perspiration beaded up on her face. She had heard that voice before. That soft, raspy whisper belonged to her torturer.

Emily stumbled into the bathroom and swallowed hard to keep from vomiting. She ran cold water over her face and then used the toilet. Fear was overwhelming her, and she wondered if she could walk back out the door. Taking a deep breath and walking quickly, she was grateful that Elliot and Brian were no longer in the hallway. As she sat down next to Shane, the look of panic on her face was obvious.

"What's wrong," he whispered, not wanting to call attention to her.

"I have to get out of here," she said, barely audible. "I feel sick. I have to leave this minute." The pair thanked the hostess, said that Emily wasn't feeling well, and left the party. Once outside, she frantically told Shane what she had heard and what she knew for certain to be the voice of her abductor. Shane called his supervisor. Before an hour had passed, Emily was interviewed by the BCA and a warrant had been issued to search Brian's pole barn and home; it would be conducted the next morning.

Brian was taken aback and quite irritated when the sheriff and members of the BCA showed up at his house on Johnson Lake early the next day. Cheryl wanted total privacy and never welcomed visitors of any kind. Emerson was a friendly sort of a law officer, and Brian had never had any run-ins with him. They had worked together on many city projects that needed money raised to be completed. The sheriff told Brian that the victim had implicated him in her attack and kidnapping. Brian tried to act calm as he mentally reviewed his options. "I'd better call my attorney," he said turning pale and feeling faint.

The search of the house didn't turn up anything, and they were soon moving on to the pole barn. Brian's attorney stressed to him as fervently as he could not to say a word. "Remain silent," he said. "You have nothing to hide." Brian hoped it was true.

After the investigators left, Cheryl was angry with, and frightened for, her husband. "I hope you have cleaned your shed with a tooth brush. There had better not be one trace of that woman in the entire area or you are dead meat."

Brian was crying now, and she wrapped her arms around him. "I'll do everything I can to help you, but you two have crossed the line." Cheryl was crying now, too, and wishing there was actually something she could do to protect him. She had always believed they had found consenting adults on line and had met for rough and sadistic sex. The pictures she had found in Brian's jacket told a different story. She had feared for that woman's life.

After Emily had been rescued, Cheryl had searched Brian's closet and had found many pictures of women tied up; they all had that same look of terror on their faces. Did they ever leave the pole barn? She hoped so but wasn't sure of anything at this point. Cheryl had burned every photo.

Brian was on the phone talking to his partner in crime. She could hear him saying "Thank God we cleaned that building from one end to the other. They won't find a hair or trace of anything in there."

Indeed, the forensic investigators found nothing. They had covered that building from top to bottom and found nothing suspicious—no hint of women being held there or anything else that might have lead them to believe that anyone had been murdered in the building.

CHAPTER 32

"Who Are You?"

———◆———

Shane couldn't believe he was back in Hidden Rapids to investigate murders. Prior to early last June, he hadn't returned in years; yet here he was again. His visits during the summer and then continuing into fall and winter had been amazing. He had not only renewed old friendships with a few guys but had been lucky enough to reacquaint himself with a girl he had been in love with for years.

Okay, enough reminiscing. He had a job to do. Shane pulled the mask over his nose and slowly unzipped the green plastic body bag. He had opened many similar bags in his days as a medical examiner but was never quite ready for what he would see. This body was no different from many he had examined over the years, but a sad feeling always engulfed him when he began the autopsy of an unknown person.

"Who are you?" he quietly asked the skeleton on the table. "Where did you come from and where were you going? Who loved you and misses you?" Asking those questions made him feel ready to take on the task of looking over every inch of the body, or, as in this case, the bones of an unidentified human being. He felt somewhat intrusive as he began.

Shane counted on his natural curiosity to help him with his investigations. He had been considered nosy as a child. He had asked what his parents and friends thought to be never-ending questions about everything that happened in and around his life and almost everything that went on with others also. Some questions were thought to be inappropriate, particularly by adults. His few friends were more accepting of his prying for information.

Normally before conducting an autopsy, medical examiners gather all the information they can about the subject and the events leading to their deaths. They consult medical records, doctors, friends, and family members. This exam was different. He knew there was someone out there missing a loved one, wondering what had happened. He would hope to find this person's family and give them answers. This body was void of flesh. A small hunk of brown hair hung tightly on the left side of the skull. Its teeth were still in place, but one eye socket had been crushed. It would be difficult to find the cause of death, although tooth or bone tissue could perhaps be used for identification.

Shane would name her Allie. He always named the unknown, wanting more than just a Jane Doe for the paperwork. He thought about the body lying on the table. Someone—maybe many—loved this person. His assignment in Hidden Rapids would constitute a lengthy investigation and would include many autopsies with unknown bodies. Assigning names would help him keep them straight. He knew that at least four bodies had been found, and the crime bureau was still digging. What had seemed to be a small family cemetery where a dozen or so family members had been buried over the years was becoming a convenient burial ground for a serial killer—or perhaps killers. Shane carefully put the remains back into the green bag and wrote the name Allie on the label.

Shane greeted a deputy. He was bringing in another bag with a new victim to examine. This body was more intact, a more recent prey. As Shane looked the woman over, he could tell she may not have been killed recently; her body was better preserved. Shane named her Beth and spoke to her as if she were able to answer his questions. "Where did you come from, little lady?" He moved her head slowly from one side to the other to get an overall look. She was tall...long legs and a short torso. Beth had a look of elegance about her. Although partially decayed, her body had been cared for. It had perhaps been kept for the pleasure of the perpetrator for a longer period of time. Shane knew about necrophilia; it was actually more prevalent than the public would want to know.

The person responsible for this would have to know about preserving bodies. There was a time when only a doctor, medical examiner, or a mortician would be privy to that procedure, but the Internet had many sites from which to gain that information. Getting the proper material to preserve would take a bit more work but was still feasible.

Shane weighed and measured the body. While he spoke into a recorder, he noted Beth's clothing and characteristics, such as eye color, sex, hair color and length, ethnicity, and possible age. He searched for scars, injuries, gunpowder, and other residue.

Beth had been tortured. Her teeth were gone and her body was badly bruised. One breast had been removed. Her lower torso had been badly burned. Her throat had been slit. Remnants of an elegant red blouse and long white skirt were still visible. There was enough fabric to see that there was nothing casual about her clothing. Maybe she had been at a party before she was killed.

The BCA would check missing persons from the surrounding area and hopefully find a match after DNA samples were processed. The other skulls he had examined so far contained teeth. DNA could be extracted from them. In 2014 the BCA had received a grant from the National Institute of Justice to use technology that allowed forensic scientists to test samples from human remains against potential relatives. Shane knew that in these cases, even though they were dealing with old samples, DNA technology had greatly improved and may help them identify the victims.

Shane thought of popular crime dramas on television where good-looking super-sleuths solve their cases with uncanny swiftness. They are portrayed as being able to obtain detailed information from the tiniest clues. He continued the slow, painstaking procedure, recording everything on the body diagram and in verbal notes. Shane made the

Y-shaped incision as he began the abdominal and chest examination. Next he would examine the organs, using a rib cutter to access organs.

A seasoned pathologist, Shane freed the intestines by cutting along the attachment tissue. The abdominal examination was time-consuming, and he did not want to rush. There were going to be many bodies, and this case was going to be a newsworthy item, no doubt picked up by state and national media. There would be intense scrutiny of the bureau's handling of the investigation. Prominent locals would be involved, and Shane expected criticism by attorneys when—if—charges were brought. The nitpicking would be widespread, and he was determined to follow strict protocol with each autopsy. There would be no short cuts in his work.

He thought of himself as a detective in his job with the bureau. A forensics detective, investigating and asking questions about everything, was his calling. He savored any puzzle and his chase to solutions.

As he examined the organs and took tissue samples, he thought again of the young woman lying on the stainless steel table. She had a story to tell, and he planned to be the eyes that would see that story play out. Sectioning some of the organs for further testing, he spoke to the body. "Who are you? I'm naming you Beth, but someday I'll know who you really are. I'll find your family, and they will put you to rest."

A tear rolled silently down the side of his face. He typically could separate himself from his job, but today it had been particularly difficult. Shane now made a cut with a saw across the crown of her head, from the boney bump behind one ear to the bump behind the other. He placed the brain tissue in formalin. Shane would leave it there for a few days while it preserved the organ and changed the consistency of the tissue, making it easier to examine.

When his inspection and samples of the organs were completed, he placed them in bags to prevent leakage and returned most of them to the body, including the breastbone and ribs. He lined the body with cotton wool and closed it with the characteristic baseball stitch.

Shane's back was killing him and daylight was ending. He would call it a day and go back to his motel. Switching from Shane Connelly, detective and forensic scientist, to Shane Connelly, the ordinary person, was never easy. Work consumed most of his life, and the transition to a social being took some concentration.

Shane had grown up in Hidden Rapids, but it felt strange to be here for this assignment. His parents had passed away years before, and he had had no reason to return. The friends he had in high school had scattered to other parts of the country. They occasionally met in places like Las Vegas or New York for mini reunions. The presence of a serial killer in his hometown was difficult to wrap his mind around.

The area had changed in those intervening years. He had returned for an all-school reunion in the summer and several times in recent months to spend time with Emily at the resort. As he drove to the motel, he still felt like a total stranger. He was often in cities where he knew no one, which didn't bother him; but here he had felt lonely—left out— not belonging. He didn't like it. He hated the idea of a murderer in his hometown. His growing love for Emily was changing his mindset though. He now felt a certain excitement about being back in his child-hood territory, and he hoped he would soon feel at home again.

He had enjoyed his return for the school reunion, but that was only for a weekend and he hadn't taken the time to drive around. The down-town was so different, and the arrival of so many new businesses seemed mind-boggling. Nothing stays the same. He knew that. But because he hadn't been around to watch the growth, it felt surreal—almost as if he hadn't lived here for 18 years. Maybe he'd stop for a cold one at the Beachcomber before settling into his motel room.

The parking lot by the motel was full. It couldn't just be the motel customers' vehicles he thought. It could, of course, be the delicious food the dining room was famous for, or, the lounge was popular, too. He'd check it out. He called Emily to ask if she would join him. "You bet!" she replied, "and may I invite Stone and Kirsten, too? We're all sitting out on the deck."

The Beachcomber was filled with men sporting beards, short-sleeved shirts, and Levis. The women, who were dressed casually in tee shirts, shorts, and flip flops, chatted with friends as the sounds of laughter and ice clinking in glasses filled the lounge.

Shane walked to the bar and sat on a tall swivel stool. He ordered a Jack Daniel's. "Water, no ice." He swiveled his chair around so he could watch the crowd sitting at the tables and searched the face of every person, looking for hints of familiarity. He tried to remember the classmates who had stayed in Hidden Rapids after high school. The main jobs in the area were with the paper company or the DNR. A few classmates had returned with teaching degrees and were now with the Hidden Rapids school system. An accountant or two had returned to open businesses in Itasca County.

He had talked to classmates at the reunion who had remained in the area; Shane was trying hard to remember who they were. He had found it interesting and even fun to connect with old friends. The three joining him walked in with smiles and greetings for him. Emily and Kirsten's hugs and Stone's handshake made him feel quite at home.

CHAPTER 33

"Put It Off Until Tomorrow— You've Hurt Me Enough Today"

———

THE NEXT MORNING SHANE WAS back on his job trying to identify murdered women. He named the third young girl Connie. That cadaver resembled the previous one almost identically. After painstaking examination of the body and note taking, another green bag was carried in.

Body number four arrived. Shane named her Delilah. She was encased in a casket and well preserved. *A mortician or at least someone who knew about body preservation had taken care of this body,* Shane surmised. She was dressed for a party. A green flowing dress with a slit up to her thigh and a white and green cape surrounded her slight frame. Her makeup had been added recently. Shane hated to presume because it felt too weird, but then he worked in a sometimes-bizarre world. Delilah's body may have been used for someone's pleasure on a regular basis. After checking with forensic scientists in charge of the excavations, he discovered that the ground around this body was quite soft. It had been worked recently.

Although nothing had been found at the site of Brian's pole barn, Shane and his co-workers were suspicious of Elliot as well. Perhaps the pole barn was not where the victims had been held captive, but a judge did issue a search warrant for Elliot's residence and the funeral home.

Brittany was appalled at the thought of strangers rummaging through their belongings. What seemed like an army of investigators descended on their home. She grew hysterical as they riffled through her kitchen cabinets, dresser drawers, bathroom medicine cabinets, and vanities. As her beds were torn apart and the mattresses pulled to the floor, she had to be restrained.

The funeral home was right next door. An adjoining walkway led to the office; and through the office door were a number of rooms for viewings and prayer services. That search was a forensic nightmare. The number of people who had come and gone out of the building had left a blur of DNA.

The preparation room had stainless steel tables that were spotlessly clean. Drains were swabbed without much hope of finding any usable evidence. The two bodies being prepared for viewing were checked but in essence not bothered. With the search about to end, one of the men looked suspiciously at a large file cabinet in one of the offices. The wall behind it looked slightly different, and nudging the cabinet revealed a door. Opening the door revealed a small room. There, under a blanket, was a white coffin. Inside laid a pretty young woman dressed totally in pink.

The BCA team was called and immediately descended on the funeral home. Elliot was asked about the discovery and mumbled something about holding the body until next of kin could plan the funeral. Shane was already busy taking samples of the body when Elliot's attorney arrived. This could very well be the 'killing room'. A closet at the far end of the room stored long dresses, skirts, silk camisoles, sweaters, nylons, women's underwear, and shoes. Heavy straps and a large supply of colored duct tape lined a table with at least a hundred different colors of nail polish. Emory boards, soap, and nail clippers sat as if waiting for the next victim to be brought to this room of horror.

Elliot had called Brian the minute the hidden room had been found. Brian was with a customer, but the tone in Elliot's voice was pure fright, and Brian had quickly excused himself. The words that tumbled out of Elliot's mouth sent panic through Brian. He abruptly left the bank and drove home. Cheryl was mowing the lawn when he came running toward her; she knew something was dreadfully wrong.

"They found the dead body in the funeral home!" Brian screamed. Cheryl suppressed a laugh; there probably *would* be dead bodies in a mortuary.

She shut down the mower, got off, and walked over to where Brain was now throwing up, his words incoherent as he tried to wipe the vomit off his face.

"Settle down," she said rolling her eyes and throwing up her arms. "Let's talk about this crisis that has you in such hysterics."

Brian sobbed as they walked the short distance to the house.

"What is it? Are you ill? Dying? Or what?" she asked.

"I'm going to prison."

"Why in the world are you going to prison?" she asked, seeing his despair and believing something had happened to scare him absolutely to death.

"The woman," he said, spitting out the words as though they had been stuck in his throat. "They found the woman that Elliot had saved in the funeral home."

"Saved? What do you mean 'saved'? Saved from what?"

"Saved for himself—saved to have sex with whenever he wants."

Cheryl began to feel nauseated. How could she have heard those words from a man she loved and trusted with her life?

"Brian, try to calm down and tell me what's been going on. I know you meet people online. I know you and Elliot like rough sex—but murder?" She was shouting and pacing around the living room. "I can't believe it! It was Elliot, wasn't it? He talked you into his craziness."

"Elliot killed the women who were found in my family's cemetery, but I was a part of it, too. I didn't do the killing, but I knew it was going to happen. Sometimes I watched."

Composing himself, Brian declared, "I can't go to prison. I'll die there the first week."

Cheryl strongly sensed he intended to take his own life.

"Wait—just wait a minute. We'll call our attorney. Surely he can help. There must be something we can do." Cheryl was pleading now.

"The fire should have killed Roxanne. If that blaze had done its job, she would be dead. The lakeshore would never have been sold. The trenchers wouldn't have unearthed the bodies. I'm insane. You know that Cheryl. You've known that for a long time. I've tried to control myself but it never worked. The urges…the moon…I can't control myself when the moon is full."

"Don't blame it on the moon!" Cheryl shouted. "It was Elliot! That demented fool must have forced you into helping him. Please, please just wait until morning." She had regained control of her emotions and needed time to think. "At least give me one more night with you, and then we'll talk about our options."

Cheryl had prayed that he was not involved when the bodies were being dug up. She hadn't wanted to talk about it with Brian. She didn't *want* to hear what he might tell her. Today she had no choice. There was no more denying, no more pretending, that there wasn't a monster living in the person she had called her husband for many years. They lay in their bed with arms wrapped around each other, finally drifting into a restless sleep.

In the early morning, Brian moved slowly off the bed and walked quietly into the kitchen. His very existence had scrolled through his mind most of the night. Memories of a full moon and uncontrollable urges haunted him. Elliot had been affected by the same demons. They had paired up early in youth after the entrance of the Ruler.

Brian remembered the ancient philosopher Seneca's quote: "Malice drinks half of its own poison." He drank that poison after learning of Cheryl's love for Stone. He had done his best to frame Stone for the abduction of the three missing girls. Their disappearance would have nothing to do with the full moon, but Elliot was willing to help even without the influence of the moon. He hadn't succeeded in sending Stone to prison, but he had destroyed his reputation. He had successfully diverted all suspicions toward Stone so he could no longer comfortably come home to the place he loved and where his family had lived.

Now, Brian supposed the missing girls would be, perhaps already had been, found in the uncovered graves. However, he wasn't afraid because his tortured life would soon be over...at his own hand.

Daylight woke Cheryl, and she reached for Brian. Just as she realized he wasn't next to her, she heard the gunshot. Leaping out of bed, she saw his body lying on the kitchen floor. On the table was a note that merely said, "We are out of options."

CHAPTER 34

"DIRTY LITTLE SECRET"

———◆———

ELLIOT HAD NOT BEEN CHARGED so far, but he knew that would be coming. Brittany was incensed but had finally stopped screaming and flailing on the floor. The sedative was wearing off and another was definitely needed. She still didn't *get it*, didn't understand Elliot's motivation for keeping the dead woman's body. Brittany, for at least a while, had believed Elliot's statement about keeping the corpse for a family. There were times when a person's remains had been kept until a burial could be arranged. One time in particular came to mind when the son of a deceased woman spent his winter in Texas and internment had been postponed until spring. Elliot had kept the woman's corpse frozen for months. However, this one was not being kept on ice.

Brittany's babble about the search, her humiliation, and the disruption of not only her things but her life in general began to reach deep into Elliot's psyche. The annoying triviality of her complaints felt like finger nails scraping on a chalkboard.

Brittany threw ice into a glass and poured herself a large brandy. She sat down, crossed her legs, and stared at her husband. She smugly asked Elliot, "Why was that dead woman hidden away in a room I knew nothing about, and who were you keeping her for?"

"For myself," he answered bluntly.

"Why?" she asked, drawing out her simple question.

"I used her for pleasure," he yelled, "Did you hear me?"

"Gratification with a dead person? With a corpse?" Brittany screamed, then gagged.

"I had *pleasure* with lots of corpses. They were my lovers, my mistresses."

"Stop!" Brittany's face was ashen. "No more! You are insane!"

"Yes, I know I am," he whispered. "I tried as hard as I could to quit, but I couldn't. I was too weak. Brian had it, too, but he didn't want satisfaction with dead people. He wanted them alive and to paint their nails first."

"Brian was a party to this? Good Gawd! I am living in an insane asylum with a lunatic," Brittany shouted. "Am I safe from you or are you going to kill me, too?"

"I should have killed you years ago, but I loved you too much, and I still do. I tried every day to keep you somewhat happy. I just wanted you to love me like you did when we first got married."

"You forced me to stay here," Brittany said, glaring into Elliot's face, "to live in this one-horse town. You refused to give me the prestige of being a doctor's wife. I had *expected* to be a doctor's wife. That's *who* I married."

"I am truly sorry for that. My father wanted, no…expected, me to be in the business with him. I just couldn't say no. "Plus," he went on, "I was not cut out to be a doctor. I could go through all the motions but I never wanted to be one. I'm too much like my father. He too enjoyed corpses. I saw him—it was horrible—unspeakable—then tempting—ultimately, exhilarating."

"I've heard enough," Brittany said and started to leave the room where they had been talking.

"Oh, no," Elliot sneered and blocked her way. "I have much more to tell you, much more that you are going to hear."

"I'm leaving this room," she declared and tried to push him out of the way. He stopped her, swiftly pushing her down hard into a chair.

"You're not leaving," he said with determination. "I'm telling you what I've been doing, and you *are* going to listen."

He held her arms down, leaning over her with his hands on her wrists while he told the tale of brutal murders and torture over the last many years. He explained that the first murder was actually Brian's idea. He went on to give details of Brian's jealousy of Stone and the plot to frame him. They had grabbed a woman Stone had been with as she got out of her car in front of her apartment. There was no one around, and it was exciting. Taking her to the funeral home's hidden room stirred their impulses and quirky desires. Brian had painted her nails, then Elliot joined in.

He went on to say they had preferred to meet their *lovers* online. The women, and sometimes men, liked the netherworld. The people they met either lived in the shadows, engaging in prostitution, or had two lives: either mingling with God-fearing, ordinary people, or lurking about, secretly seeking depravity. They didn't murder all the people they met on the Internet. Elliot had twisted sex with live women, too.

Brittany pleaded for him to stop telling her about the perverted sex he and Brian had been having with prostitutes or free and easy women. He gave her a disgusted look and continued his story. She *was* going to hear it all before this came to an end.

Elliot finally got tired of leaning over and hanging on to her. He let her go, threatening to hold her down again if she tried to leave the room.

His story of unnatural desires and the full moon's pull repulsed her. Elliot seemed convinced that the Devil's strangle hold on him and the phases of the moon forced him into his lascivious behavior. He told her he planned to end his life, to take a lethal pill. It would be fast and painless. After he told her she could go, Brittany bolted out of the room, ran to her bedroom, and locked the door. She buried herself under the covers and sobbed with fear and disgust. Her thoughts were also of the disgrace and humiliation she would have to face. She would leave town as quickly as possible. The fact that her husband was in the other bedroom very possibly dying was of no consequence to her.

CHAPTER 35

"God Be with You till We Meet Again"

———◆———

Darlene Hayes, Susan Timmons, Kathy Sanders, Yvette Hunter, Juanita Morales, Roberta Hawkins, and Mary Maki. Shane wrote the names slowly and carefully. He had processed these women, moved their heads or skulls around, cut deep into some of their bodies, and talked gently to them.

The lost had been found. Some were not acknowledged as lost. Some had no one who cared whether they were dead or alive, found, or lying alone in an unmarked grave forever. But now *he* knew, and *he* cared. They would have a home in death—he would see to that.

Never had Shane had this feeling of loss and of such attachment to the dead. Perhaps it was that he was in his hometown or maybe that he was just getting older, that he had seen too much and was feeling the sadness that came with the discoveries of persons no one even knew had been missing.

He retrieved his files of the women and slowly crossed off the names he had given them. Allie was actually Mary Maki; Beth was Susan Timmons. Along with the sadness came a sense of intense accomplishment, not just in his forensics work but also in the entire community's ability to join hands and work together. The unbelievable crimes, perpetrated by trusted upstanding members of the area, had forced all to realize that a dark side of human nature truly does exist.

The sophisticated network of missing persons and DNA base had made identifying the bodies possible, and their families had been notified. Many had been missing for a long time. The investigators believed the graves hid the early victims and speculated that later ones had been cremated. There was no way to know with certainty how many there had actually been.

Area residents organized a memorial service for the murdered women. It was held at the Myles Rief Center. Brittany had donated burial containers for the cremated remains. Hidden Rapids Florist donated floral bouquets for each woman. Families of the deceased had been ushered in to sit in the front rows. People of all ages attended. Some were frail; their expressions, heartbreaking.

Several members of the clergy took part in the service. The choir from Redeemer Lutheran sang "The Strife Is Over" while men and women of the Minnesota Bureau of Apprehension carried in urns and pictures of the women. Shawn led the procession. He had worked feverishly to discover the identity of the murder victims. Kirsten carried Roberta Hawkins' ashes. She was the last woman to have disappeared.

Families and the community now gazed with dismay at the pictures of the young victims. The framed images sitting on top the urns seemed to stare back. Some were of the women as children; recent pictures of them as young women could not be found. Sadness shrouded the gathering as a young woman's voice filled the center with the song, "I Will Remember You—Will You Remember Me?"

The reading from Isaiah 43: 1-3 comforted the mourners:

And He who formed you, Oh Israel: Fear not for I have redeemed you; I have called you by your name; you are mine. When you pass through the water, I will be with you; and through the rivers, they shall not overflow you. When you walk through the fire, you shall not be burned.

The pastor from First Lutheran assured everyone that God had been with the women and that they had not walked through the valley of dcath alone. The large assembly of people stumbled through the words of the Twenty-third Psalm. Sobs filled the center.

A family member of one of the women had been chosen to speak for the families of the victims. He thanked the community on behalf of all the relatives. He talked of finally having answers to questions that had for so many years plagued his parents and the parents of so many of the missing. The fact that they could give a proper burial to their loved ones gave them closure.

Judge Chantal McAllister—as beautiful, well known, and admired as ever—had caught the eye of many as she walked in with a striking, elderly woman. Chantal had myriad thoughts racing through her brain. She thought she was so lucky to have escaped with her life from the clutches of Brian Abbott. If he had been in the mood to share her with Elliot that particular summer night, she would have been dead.

CHAPTER 36

"GOT AN ANGEL ON MY SHOULDER"

———◆———

THE DRAMA THAT HAD HELD the entire community in suspense was over. Brian had taken his own life, and Elliot, too, had taken the coward's way out. Emily was now making arrangements to meet with her own personal conspirators. Kirsten, whose pretensions of being Jenny had forced Emily to relive her torment; her father, who had been an active participant in the deception; Billie, who, knowing how Emily loved the lake and their cabin, had lured her into spending time in Hidden Rapids by offering her a job remodeling the cabins; and Stone, even Stone, who had become close friends with Shane and Emily, had been a part of the deceit.

Emily had explored her soul, had asked herself the hard questions, and had answered a few with what she believed was an enlightened spirit. She believed that her father and Billie had been interested in both her well being and Josh's. She still, however, couldn't help but feel used and betrayed.

They gathered at Stonebridge. Billie had pleaded for a neutral and calm setting. She was well aware of Emily's anger at everyone involved and understood. The lazy flame in the fireplace lent a tranquil feeling to the group settling into the lodge's great room. A few appetizers sat on a round table she had set up. Several bottles of wine had been opened with Billie offering a glass to quiet the nerves. Shane accompanied Emily and sat next to her, holding her hand. Paul began talking, trying hard to explain his participation in the scheme. Emily already trusted his love and knew he wouldn't hurt her, but she still questioned his actions.

Billie now spoke to justify her trying to keep Emily in Hidden Rapids. She did not know the storage room at the resort had played a big part in Emily's terror. Billie had absolutely no idea of the horror that had played out in the back yard of Stonebridge. The knowledge that her husband, Jenny's father, had been a spectator to his own daughter's murder was more than she could absorb. His freakish car accident was no longer a mystery.

The person that Emily had the hardest time forgiving was Kirsten. They had become close friends, yet Kirsten had deceived her. Emily had questions for her.

"Yours was the voice on the phone?" Emily asked as she stared into Kirsten's eyes.

"Yes," Kirsten answered, forcing herself to look at Emily. "I was doing my job," she said, dropping her eyes to the floor.

"Well then, you have a lousy job!" Emily replied angrily.

"Were you also the woman in the gauzy white dress at the cemetery?" Emily shook her head in disbelief as she asked the question.

"Yes. I followed you to the cemetery and parked my car just below the hill. I lingered on the edge, not too close and just long enough for you to see me. Then I disappeared down the hill and drove away."

Perturbed, Emily asked, "How did you brush your cold hand across my face without my seeing you."

"I didn't!" Kirsten said indignantly. "I didn't touch your face or any other part of you. I wasn't close enough."

'I know that *someone* touched me." Emily was adamant about that.

"Well, it wasn't me."

"Did you swim with me in Pokegama and help me through the rough water?"

"Are you kidding," Kirsten laughed. "I don't even swim. I'm scared to death of water. I don't know *who* was with you, but it never would have been me."

"*I* think it *was* Jenny," Billie said, tears streaming down her face. "You said you saw her clearly in the storage room. I think she's been here with you—by your side—ever since you arrived at Stonebridge."

It could be true. Emily was positive she had seen her in the storage room. The thought of Jenny's coming to help Emily remember actually gave her comfort.

By the time the discussions were finished, forgiveness filled the room. Emily and Kirsten hugged and cried. Stone too expressed his regret at the deception that had gone on. He had been under suspicion for so long and was willing to go along with almost anything to have the mystery solved.

Emily felt peaceful entering the cemetery. Her mom's grave was covered with the flowers that she and her father had brought the week before in remembrance of her mother's birthday. Today she was alone with her thoughts. Emily had found serenity and loved the way it had seemed to wrap her in comfort. The road to discovery had been long and arduous. Emily had called on and found strength she never believed she had. Her journey had been tough, but she had been tougher.

Shane had been her rock, and she had leaned long and hard on him. They had fallen in love and decided to marry. There was no date set, but the engagement ring that glistened on her finger was a promise.

She walked over to the other grave where another loved one laid. Jenny's spirit was free. Emily could feel it. There was no unfinished business, no restless force moving about. Emily believed without a doubt that Jenny had come to her, had protected her and pressed her to remember so her soul could be at peace.

Emily started walking back to her car when she spotted another visitor to the graveyard. It was the same woman she had seen on her first visit, a visit where Kirsten had appeared in a white dress and Jenny had brushed a cold hand across her face. She hadn't known her then but certainly knew her now. She had been her rescuer, her savior from death at the hands of Elliot and Brian.

Cheryl saw Emily and hurriedly started to walk away. "Please, let me speak to you, Cheryl," Emily pleaded. Cheryl stopped and waited for Emily to get to her. "I just want to thank you. You saved my life."

"I'm glad I found you in time," the hesitant heroine replied. "I'm sorry I didn't just take you to the hospital and let the chips fall where they may. I was a coward and I wanted to protect my husband."

"It's okay. I got out of there, thanks to you," Emily tried not to gush but wanted Cheryl to know that she was fully aware of the battle she would have had with her conscience.

Cheryl went on to say that that was the one and only time Brian and Elliot had used the pole barn for a captive. There had been too much going on in the funeral home to use it at that time, but it had normally been the place for torture and murder. The pole barn was the first place she had thought of after seeing Emily's picture, and she would not have known where else to look. Cheryl said that she would not have thought of the funeral home.

"How did you find the picture of me?" Emily was curious.

"I walked by Brian's coat and it had fallen off the chair it was hanging on. Nothing touched it but it just fell on the floor and I picked it up. The top of the picture was sticking out."

"It was my angel, Jenny. She made it fall. She knew you would save me." Emily smiled at Cheryl's look of bewilderment.

Emily went on to tell Cheryl about her and Josh remembering Jenny's murder and of the protection she felt Jenny had given her. Emily also recalled the story in the paper recently about an 18-month-old toddler who survived 14 hours strapped in a car seat upside down in a river in Utah. The rescuers reported a woman's voice calling out, "Help me, help me," as they arrived on the scene. The mother was already dead. Was it a voice from the dead? From Heaven? The rescuers believed it was the child's mother calling to them.

"Well," Cheryl said, as they walked to their cars. "You're blessed. You have an angel on your shoulder looking out for you."

Roxanne would soon discover she had an angel as well. Her mental disorder was now under control, and she was eager to show off her beautiful new home. She had planned a party for Saturday, and it was to be a gala affair. Roxanne was preparing to have ten guests for dinner. The weather was predicted to be warm and sunny. Lake Pokegama would be at its best.

Steaks sat ready to go on the grill, potatoes baked in the oven, and Roxanne put the final ingredients to a crunchy lettuce salad. Cheese, crackers, pretzels, dipping sauces, pickles, and chips filled the outdoor dining table. Holly, Josh, and the grandchildren had arrived early so Holly could help her mother with last minute details. The children were already trying out the new slide that sent them sailing into the warm Pokegama water.

Kirsten, Stone, and Billie arrived together with Shane and Emily close behind. As the guests settled on the deck with cool drinks, Roxanne saw an unfamiliar car pull up next to the garage. She could not believe her eyes as she watched her ex-husband, Charles, get out and walk to the side door. Livid, she glanced quickly around to see if Jack or Holly were close by so they could deal with him. They were not, so Roxanne opened the door. Before she could scold him for coming, especially unannounced and without an invitation, he brought out a photo album.

"I know you lost everything in the fire," he said, looking uncomfortable. So I made copies of our family pictures for you." Roxanne was floored. She wanted to speak, but words wouldn't come. "Are you all right now? Holly says you are making great progress and that the two of you are spending time together." He sounded sincere and caring.

"Yes, I'm better—much better. I'm not cured and never will be, but I'm learning how to control my obsession."

"It's good to see you, Roxanne. We have three wonderful grandchildren, don't we?"

"Yes, we sure do," Roxanne replied as she reached out her hand to him. He took her hand, gently squeezed it, and walked back to his car.

A sense of utter tranquility drifted through her mind and body. She breathed a long sigh and joined her guests. She thought of Emily's belief that Jenny had been the angel on her shoulder. After the pleasant encounter she had just had with her ex husband, she wondered, *Maybe we all have angels looking out for us.*

CHAPTER 37

"Just as I am Without One Plea"

———◆———

STONE GOT THE CALL ABOUT the internment for Brian. It would be late in the day on Tuesday. Only the funeral director, Stone, and Cheryl would be present. Stone had wondered about accepting the invitation, but Cheryl had called and asked him to come. After all, he had been friends with the three men. Two were now dead—and Cheryl, whose life had once again been turned upside down.

Stone drove into the Abbott family cemetery, wary of what he was going to experience. He hadn't seen Cheryl since Brian's death and didn't know what to expect. Brian of course would be laid to rest. Stone didn't know if it would be a burial of a body or if he had been cremated and just the box with his remains would be placed into the ground. He reminded himself that it's not as if it mattered. Wrapping his mind around the events of the past year had left him in shock. He had taken a leave of absence from work and tried to understand what had actually happened. Bodies of young women had been dug up after electrical trenchers discovered the first. Fetishes and satanic rituals had riveted the community, cloaking the area in fear and revulsion.

Three people—the funeral director, Cheryl, and Reverend Markuson—were standing near a black gravestone in the center of the cemetery. Glancing at Stone, a hesitant smile formed on Cheryl's face, and Stone returned the friendly gesture. An awkward hug ensued and a breathy hello.

Brian's burial place would be next to his parents. Stone did not ask questions, but while reflecting on the past events, he had not thought Brian would be buried next to his parents, next to the hiding places for the women he had played a part in murdering. Just as the pastor was beginning to read from scripture, Jack and Roxanne came walking down the path. They stood by Stone and Cheryl while Reverend Markuson read of forgiveness from the Book of Psalms, Chapter 139, verses 7-8: *Where can I go from your spirit? Or where can I flee from your presence? If I ascend into heaven, you are there; I make my bed in hell, behold, you are there.* He talked of God's forgiveness for even the most atrocious crimes.

Forgiveness. The word rolled around in Roxanne's mind as she stood in the old cemetery. She had spent hours with her therapist, trying to come to terms with what had happened—her brother's involvement with the murdered women and the awful sight she had witnessed walking into this once restful place the day of the discovery. She would forgive—needed to forgive—her brother for his sins. He had psychological problems, too, that were more than he could handle.

The six in attendance recited The Lord's Prayer. A few minutes were needed to inter the container. "Good-bye," from the director, "God Bless," from the Reverend, and a brief hug for Cheryl from Roxanne and Jack left Stone and Cheryl looking down at the stone:

Brian Abbott
August 21, 1981 – June 15, 2015

Cheryl walked over and sat on a bench nearby. Stone hesitated for a moment, then walked over and sat down beside her. He had planned to get out of there the minute the burial was completed, but the look on her face was painful for him to see. They had been such good friends—all four of them—like brothers. They would have given their lives for each other. Or at least that's what they had believed when the four were young and fearless. What had gone on to change things so much was the question he had asked himself over and over these last months.

"I didn't dare to bury Brian in a coffin. I couldn't leave the body intact, though I would have liked to. I was afraid someone might dig him up and steal him or do something horrible with his corpse." Cheryl was distraught, weeping uncontrollably.

Stone looked deeply into her eyes. These were the same eyes he thought he had seen almost every day of his life until he graduated high school. These same eyes had watched out for him in football games, protecting him from a defensive line that sorely wanted to hurt him, to throw him on the ground. Sacking the quarterback had been their goal. The eyes that searched his face now were the same eyes that would give him a glance—a look—right before lining up. That look had said, "I'm running interference for you, Buddy. I've got your back." He could see in Cheryl's eyes his old friend Darryl. Her eyes looked exactly like his.

Was Cheryl so different? Stone stared at her now, not knowing what to say. Cheryl was not looking for words from him. She knew he was on to her. She had a story to tell, a story she had wanted to tell him for years.

"I knew I was different from the time I was a kid," Cheryl said, slowly choosing her words. "I wasn't sure what it was, but I knew I didn't exactly fit with the boys. My size gave me confidence, and no one ever messed with me. I wasn't comfortable being a guy. Yet I was so darn big. I envied Brian for his slim stature and height, and Elliot, for his dark, beautiful, thick hair and cocky attitude. I didn't envy you, Stone—I just loved you."

Stone swallowed hard and coughed nervously. "I don't know what to say," he almost whispered; he could feel a blush rising.

The sheriff had told Stone about Brian's jealousy. Cheryl's feelings of love toward Stone had prompted Brian to try and frame him. Putting Stone in prison had been Brian's long-time goal. However, hearing the words coming from Cheryl, Stone had a tough time wrapping his head around the notion. Brian had forced Stone to give up time with his family. He was trying hard to forgive Brian, the man he thought was a close friend, for trying to ruin his life as revenge for Cheryl's wanting Stone instead of himself.

"I'm still the same person," Cheryl said, playing with her hair and coaxing it behind her ears. "I lived in a seedy world when I first got out of college. I was a hotshot broker by day, making my clients pots full of money, and a deviant after dark." She looked long and hard at Stone, waiting for a reaction. "I didn't know what I was: gay? transvestite? transgender? I only knew I was miserable and depressed. I self medicated with drugs and alcohol until I finally sought help from a therapist and found my way back." As Cheryl spoke, the wind blew softly through the trees and the sound of jet skis reverberated through the small cemetery.

"I buried him here, even though the place held horror, because it was a place where I believed he would be safe. I know how ridiculous that sounds, but I did love him, too. In spite of his bizarre behavior I felt a great deal of compassion and sympathy for him."

Stone looked at the newly laid sod where trencher operators had discovered the first skeleton. The box had been cardboard and the body, decayed. The medical examiner had said it had been there over 50 years. Speculation by law enforcement was that the previous mortician, Elliot's father, had most likely been the first killer. Stone wondered why she would have chosen the site that had harbored such horror.

"I buried him here because it *is* private property," Cheryl remarked quietly, seeming to read Stone's thoughts. "No Trespassing signs have kept most inquisitive onlookers away, and Roxanne can easily obtain a restraining order if needed against intruders.

"Where've you been?" Stone questioned. "I heard you had left town."

"I've been in Minneapolis," Cheryl responded. She went on to say she knew she had to leave Hidden Rapids. She actually had not known about the murders but did know that Elliot and Brian engaged in brutal sex, although she had believed it was sex with consenting adults. Cheryl had, however, been the one to rescue Emily, and she had not come forward. Once she had found the picture of Emily and saved her from the macabre death Elliot had planned for her, she had confronted Brian but had not gone to the police.

Cheryl had changed her name and opened her own brokerage firm in Minneapolis. Again, she was making money for her clients. She had changed her name to Christine. It was her grandmother's name. She went on to say that since her education records had all been under the name of Darryl, she had had them changed after her surgery to Cheryl. This time she had started her own business again and no one had yet asked to see her diploma. Her clients now were mostly old friends from her college days and early working career. She had made them money no matter what name he (or she) had used; they simply did not care.

"I'm hungry," Stone declared. "Let's stop by the Beachcomber and have a burger." Cheryl's face showed delight. "Yes," she said, surprised by the suggestion. "I'd like that."

The parking lot was full of cars, and Stone wondered if they would find a place to sit. Entering the bar, the noisy crowd hushed as the two found a couple of empty chairs. People stared and whispered. A waitress walked over and, with a smile, asked what she could get for them.

"I'll have a beer," Stone answered, and Cheryl ordered the same. When the beers arrived, Stone quietly proposed a toast. "To old friends," he murmured. Cheryl smiled, nodded her head, and they clinked their glasses.

When the pair had enjoyed a burger and a beer, they left the bar. Stone hugged Cheryl hard. "Let's keep in touch," Stone suggested.

"Yes," Cheryl said and showed that same old smirk Stone had seen a million times. "Yes, let's do that." They shook hands, then hugged, said their good-byes, and each left feeling good about the day.

CHAPTER 38

"Count Your Blessings"

Stories of the macabre murders no longer smeared the front pages of the newspapers and weren't the constant morning coffee talk in the restaurants. They still came up in conversations, but there were other events that seemed to take the edge off of what had been a ghoulish parade of events.

Emily was applying the finishing touches to the new chalet at the end of the road. Paul continued to mourn the loss of his longtime love, Lucy Fox. He had taken it extremely hard at first but had always believed one reaps what one sows. Emerson's visit had revived old wounds and guilt. Her heart had given out when it was apparent she had been complicit in Jenny's death. Although she had not taken part in the murder, she had witnessed the crime and had remained silent. Emily's continued presence and having the old Josh back gave him great joy. Holly and Josh's three children gave them all a renewed sense of family.

Emily had returned to California, arranging to move to Minnesota. She and Shane were ready to begin a life together in Minnesota. After a visit to Sybil Fitzgerald, they would be on their way. The mansion had a Sold sign in the front yard. Sybil and Rita greeted them. Sybil had purchased a villa in Palm Springs. She and Rita would spend winters there and summers in Duluth close to Chantal in a quaint cottage on the shores of Lake Superior. Each home needed Emily's expert decorating skills, and Emily agreed to travel between the two places. Emily was already finding ample work in Minnesota.

Billie had recovered nicely but lacked the energy to manage the resort full time. So, Stone decided to take over. Billie would continue helping, as would Roxanne. Kirsten and Stone were in love and planned to marry.

Brittany had the funeral home bulldozed and the contents hauled away and burned. The entire episode had her in daily hysterics. Gawkers gathered every day to hurl rocks against the building and tear siding and pieces of the building off, which had put her over the edge. She changed her name and moved to a prestigious part, of course, of Florida.

Emily had planned an open house to show off the Blake's new vacation villa. Roxanne and Jack were the first to arrive. There would be a private happy hour with a few friends prior to the larger gathering and the catered meal. Close to a hundred people would tour the open house and enjoy the beach. Billie, Stone, and Kirsten walked over with wine bottles in hand. Josh and Holly pulled into the drive at the same time. The weather had cooperated and a gentle breeze blew off the clear blue water. Shane helped with appetizers as revelers filled the huge deck.

Love was in the air as Emily, Roxanne, and Kirsten talked of their engagements and wedding plans. Billie, a romantic at heart, had suggested shared nuptials on Stonebridge beach with a combined reception at the lodge. Each woman had conferred with her fiancé and all decided to accept her generous offer.

Roxanne continued to fight a daily battle with hoarding. Jack knew the gravity of her illness but loved her and wanted to be a part of her life. Roxanne faithfully continued her therapy sessions, and her personal organizer continued her unrelenting inspections. She knew what was supposed to be in the house and had the nose of a bloodhound for anything unnecessary.

Shane arrived a few minutes late with news about Chantal. She had resigned as a judge and was opening her own law practice. The northern judicial community was in shock. She would specialize in Internet crime and exploitation of minors. At least half of her cases would be *pro bono*, and she intended to work closely with the sex crime units throughout the state.

Other guests had arrived and were savoring the moderate breeze that had come up. The warm day invited many to take off their flip-flops to stroll on the sandy beach with drinks in hand. Steaks cooking on many grills sent a mouth-watering aroma floating down the shore. The ambiance was good for Emily's soul.

"Shame on the Moon"

As the evening continued, a full moon rose in the sky. Surgeons in operating rooms noticed more loss of blood during surgeries. Law enforcement officers experienced a change in the mood of drivers. Domestic violence escalated. Babies cried louder. Sleep was fitful. Mental health facilities scrutinized their patients, watching as behaviors became more anxious. A forlorn woman answered an inquiry on an adult meeting site and clicked on the name *r_u_lonesome2nite*.

Acknowledgments

—◆—

My GRATITUDE GOES TO SO many, but I must say that it's handy to have an editor in the family. For me, it's my husband's sister, Ruth Kammen Knepper. Primarily, because we live several states apart, we work together online. But while passing through our area, she and I grabbed a chance for a somewhat conventional author-editor conference once the work was almost finished. It was a great chance to roll up our sleeves, drink gallons of coffee, brainstorm, hash, and rehash possibilities and probabilities. She tells me I have thick skin. I tell her, with ALMOST every suggestion, "I like it!"

Thanks also to Shari Lanning, Linda Meyers, and Trish Torgerson Nygaard for their keen eyes and candid critiques. Ruth and I too easily miss the forest for the trees.

A special thanks to author and friend John Austin Sletten for his continued encouragement.

Only families of writers understand the challenge of living with a novelist. The process takes time, and we tend to get distracted. No one deserves my appreciation more than my husband, Ken.

QUESTIONS FOR DISCUSSION

———

1. Were you engaged in the story? How did you feel reading it—sad, disturbed, frightened, confused…?
2. Did the plot pull you in?
3. Do the main characters change by the end of the book? Do they grow, or come to know something about themselves.
4. Does the story interest you?
5. What passages strike you as insightful, even profound? Perhaps a bit of dialog that's funny or poignant.
6. Is the ending satisfying? If so, why? If not, why not…and how would you change it?
7. If you could ask the author a question, what would you ask?

51681481R00120

Made in the USA
Charleston, SC
31 January 2016